IN EARLY JUNE 1964,

the Benevolent Home for Necessitous Girls burns to the ground, and its vulnerable residents are thrust out into the world. The orphans, who know no other home, find their lives changed in an instant. Arrangements are made for the youngest residents, but the seven oldest girls are sent on their way with little more than a clue or two to their pasts and the hope of learning about the families they have never known. On their own for the first time in their lives, they are about to experience the world in ways they never imagined...

Innocent

ERIC WALTERS

ORCA BOOK PUBLISHERS

Library and Archives Canada Cataloguing in Publication

Walters, Eric, 1957–, author
Innocent / Eric Walters.
(Secrets)

Issued in print, electronic and audio disc formats.
ISBN 978-1-4598-0665-8 (pbk.).—ISBN 978-1-4598-0666-5 (pdf).—
ISBN 978-1-4598-0667-2 (epub).—ISBN 978-1-4598-1094-5 (audio disc)

I. Title. II. Series: Secrets (Victoria, B.C.)
PS8595.A598I55 2015   jC813'.54   C2015-901735-1
C2015-901736-X   C2015-901737-8

First published in the United States, 2015
Library of Congress Control Number: 2015935524

Summary: In this YA novel, Betty starts to investigate her mother's murder and uncovers a sinister connection to the wealthy family she works for.

Orca Book Publishers is dedicated to preserving the environment and has printed this book on Forest Stewardship Council® certified paper.

Orca Book Publishers gratefully acknowledges the support for its publishing programs provided by the following agencies: the Government of Canada through the Canada Book Fund and the Canada Council for the Arts, and the Province of British Columbia through the BC Arts Council and the Book Publishing Tax Credit.

Cover design by Teresa Bubela
Cover images by Dreamstime.com and Shutterstock.com
Author photo by Sofia Kinachtchouk

ORCA BOOK PUBLISHERS
www.orcabook.com

Printed and bound in Canada.

18 17 16 15 • 4 3 2 1

For Anita

One

THE SUN WAS beating down on me so brightly that I had to keep my eyes tightly closed. It felt *so* good. I was like a cat basking in the sun, drinking in the warmth, letting it soak in and fill me up. I could lie here all day. Soft sand under me, the sound of the ocean in my ears... all I needed was for the breeze to be a little bit stronger. The warmth was building and becoming too hot. The smell of the ocean was changing. Had somebody started a bonfire on the beach? Why would they do that on such a beautiful, sunny day? The smell of the fire got stronger and stronger until it wasn't just in my nose. I could almost taste the smoke and—I sat bolt upright in bed. The beach was gone, but the smell remained.

I looked around, trying to make sense of my surroundings. It was almost pitch black, but in the dim light coming from the window, I could make out thin lines of smoke. Smoke...that meant there was a fire!

I tried to jump out of bed, but my feet got tangled in the covers and I tumbled to the floor, the wind knocked out of me. Frantically I kicked at the blankets, terrified and desperate to get untangled. I struggled free and scrambled on all fours, bumping into the night table, reaching up for the lamp. I grabbed it and pushed the button, but nothing happened. I pushed the button again and again, but it wasn't working!

I pulled myself to my feet. The smoke was getting thicker. I stumbled over to Toni's bed.

"Toni, Toni! Wake up, get up!"

She didn't budge. What was wrong? Without thinking, I reached down and slapped her across the face. Her eyes shot open. Even in the dim light, I could see a look of complete confusion and terror on her face.

"There's a fire!" I screamed. "Something is on fire!"

She didn't move. She looked completely stunned.

"There's smoke, a fire," I stammered. I had to make her understand.

Suddenly the look of confusion changed to panic. She was like a wild animal clutching at me, flailing her arms. I stepped back, afraid she was going to hit me. Instead, she grabbed my nightgown and held on.

"We have to get out," she yelled.

She was still holding on to my nightgown as I pulled her to her feet, out the door and into the hall. There was more smoke out there, much more.

Toni froze.

"We have to make sure *everybody* gets out! Go—pound on doors!" I said.

Her eyes were still panic-filled, but she nodded her head and let go of my nightgown.

"Fire! Fire! Fire!" Joe, the cook, was yelling from somewhere down below.

"Get Cady, get Malou...make sure they're up!" I screamed.

Toni stood there, unmoving, as if she couldn't even command her feet to walk.

"Go!" I pushed her hard, propelling her down the hall as I started in the other direction.

There was banging behind me as she hammered on a door and called out the girls' names. I reached the second door and was about to pound on it when it popped open and Sara and Dot tumbled out, bumping me into the wall. We stared at each other, speechless. I opened my mouth to say something when Joe called out again, "Fire, fire, fire!"

"We have to get out," Dot yelled.

"Yes, yes, we have to get everybody out. Go wake up Tess—she has to get out."

"She's up...she's out. She didn't come home last night," Sara said.

My mind raced, glad that she was safe, wondering why she hadn't come home, where she was and—

Toni, Malou and Cady ran down the hall and pushed the three of us ahead of them. We stumbled down the stairs, bare feet pounding against the wood. It was almost pitch dark in the windowless stairwell, but we had walked up and down the stairs so many times over the years that we didn't need light to find our way. We hit the second floor together. The smell of smoke was strong, but I still couldn't see any fire.

The door to the little-girls' dormitory was already open, and Joe and Miss Webster appeared. In Joe's arms were two of the littlest girls. Miss Webster held two more by their hands. Trailing behind Joe were the others, moving two by two and holding hands the way we'd practiced in fire drills. If only this were a drill. The girls had fear in their eyes; some were whimpering, and some had started to cry.

"Quick now, ladies!" Joe called out. "Toni, Betty, all of you big girls go down—show them the way! That's right. Good girls!"

He made it sound like this really wasn't anything more than a drill.

As a group, we went down the steps. The sound of our feet thumping down the worn stairs was all we could hear.

We reached the bottom, spread out and lined the front-hall walls. Like magic, Tess appeared, already holding the hand of one of the little girls. Unlike us, she was already dressed. Dot threw her arms around Tess as the little girls, led by Joe as if he were the Pied Piper, came down the stairs. We allowed them to pass. Through the dining hall and to the door they marched. When Miss Webster appeared at the end of the line, we followed her, our feet thundering as we crossed the verandah and ran onto the lawn. Our bare feet sank into the wet grass, and a rush of cold, fresh air entered my lungs.

Suddenly, Mrs. Hazelton, our matron, appeared. She was in her nightgown as well, standing with Joe and Miss Webster and the Little Ones. She called out for everybody to be calm, to move away from the building. As always, she was in charge, and we followed her orders. Outside, the full moon and the stars bathed the lawn in light, and I could see clearly. I kept moving away from the building, as if it were in pursuit, and I could see that we had to get farther away. Finally, with the full expanse of the lawn and the burning house behind us, we stopped.

The Little Ones now started to sob. More fully awake, they now knew enough to be scared. A pair of the girls—Debbie and Carol—broke ranks and rushed to me.

"We're all right now," I said to the girls. I swept Debbie up, and she wrapped her arms around my neck. Carol pressed against me. I knew the Little Ones needed to be comforted, but having them against me gave comfort to me as well.

"It's going to be all right," I said. I wasn't sure if I was trying to reassure them or me.

All of the other girls were spread out, scattered in groups of two or three, some standing, and some slumped to the ground. All were staring back at the house. Toni came to my side. She had two of the Little Ones clinging to her as well.

There was a chill in the air that made it seem more like early April than nearly summer. None of this seemed real. It was as if I'd woken up from a dream to find myself in a nightmare. I wanted to pinch myself and wake up from this one as well. Then I saw the flames spilling out as the fire burst through the top corner of the house. Smoke was billowing out, staining the darkened sky, making it look as if a bottle of ink had been spilled into the heavens.

I edged toward the others as they moved toward me. We seemed involuntarily drawn to huddle together. Nobody spoke as the fire roared. Now we couldn't just see it and smell it; we could hear it. The fire was consuming the house—our home, and the only home I'd ever known. The fire grew, getting louder and louder as more flames, light and smoke became visible. The whole upper floor was now engulfed, each window alive with fire. I counted over, left to right, until I found our bedroom window.

"It's there in our room," I said to Toni.

We watched as the flames engulfed it—the place where we had slept, where we had lived. Our beds, our clothing, everything we owned was being eaten by the fire.

"They'll be here soon," Toni said. "Can't you hear the fire trucks?"

I shook my head.

"We'll all be fine," she said.

"Then why are you crying?" I asked.

Toni didn't answer. She knew as well as I did that nothing was going to be fine. Even if the fire trucks arrived soon, the house was already gone.

There was an explosion, and a ball of flames shot into the air as the edge of the roof collapsed and the corner window blew out. I screamed and jumped back. Everybody else seemed to scream at the same time. I turned to Toni, but she was gone, running away across the grass, heading toward the trees and the river. I turned to go after her. She needed me, but the two little girls were clinging to me even tighter now, crying.

"Toni, come back!" I yelled, but she didn't hear me, or if she did, she didn't pay attention. I tried to take a few steps, but the little girls clung even tighter, locked in place. They needed me too. Toni would be fine. She was away from the fire.

"Is everybody here?" Mrs. Hazelton asked.

She went from person to person, looking at each one, dropping to her knees when necessary, calling out their names, counting. I thought we'd gotten them all out—unless somebody had hidden under a bed or—

"All the Little Ones are here," she said.

I felt a rush of relief flow through me. We hadn't missed anybody.

Mrs. Hazelton turned to Joe. "Could you please go down and make sure Toni is fine?"

"Yes, ma'am." He turned and left.

"The rest of you, come closer, come here, gather around." Her voice was calm, reassuring.

We all moved closer until we were pressed together almost as if we were one solid mass. It felt good. It chased away the night chill and the fear of the fire.

Mrs. Hazelton continued to speak. Her voice—that accent always made me think she was as royal as the Queen of England—was calm and reassuring. She spoke so softly that I couldn't make out all she was saying, but it still made me feel safer knowing that somehow she'd take care of the situation, take care of us, the way she always did.

The sirens had started quietly, but they were much louder now. I turned around, as did others, looking into the distance, down the road, toward town. The fire trucks were almost here.

I turned back toward our home. Flames were shooting from the roof, and thick black smoke stained the night sky, the fire throwing out light and shadows. The trucks would be here soon, but it was too late for the house. Too late for us.

Then Mrs. Hazelton's voice came again, but she wasn't talking, she was singing.

"Amazing grace! How sweet the sound
That saved a wretch like me!"

Her voice got louder with each line.

"I once was lost but now am found;
Was blind, but now I see."

Others added their voices.

"'Twas grace that taught my heart to fear
And grace my fears relieved."

More joined in—including me—and the chorus surged.

"How precious did that grace appear
The hour I first believed."

There was a tremendous crash as the entire roof collapsed, sending smoke and ash into the sky. Some of the girls screamed again.

Mrs. Hazelton's voice emerged once again, and many of us sang with her as the fire trucks rumbled up the driveway.

"Through many dangers, toils and snares,
I have already come;
'Tis grace hath brought me safe thus far,
And grace will lead me home."

Home…where would my home be?

Two

SITTING IN THE living room of Mrs. Hazelton's stone cottage, waiting outside the closed door to her study, everything seemed so normal, so calm. If it wasn't for the awful stench of smoke that still filled the air, it would be as if nothing had happened. The matron's cottage was almost all that remained on the property. Our home was a tangle of blackened, smoldering timbers, punctuated by half-burned furniture. Everything except the cottage and a nearby shed had been consumed. I was alone in the waiting room but could hear some of the other girls talking in the living room.

The door to the study opened and Toni appeared. She looked small and scared, and she wiped away some tears with the back of her hand. Toni was usually so strong that it was hard to see her cry. What had been said to her? What had happened inside that room? She was staring at a large brown envelope in her hands. Toni looked up and saw me. She tried to smile, but it came out wrong. It was small and twisted and sad, and she looked as if she was going to cry even harder.

I got to my feet and we hugged.

"I don't know what to say," she whispered in my ear, her voice raw and raspy.

"It's going to be all right," I said. Isn't that what she always said to me?

"No, you don't understand. It's—"

"Betty?" I loosened my grip on Toni and looked to the doorway where Mrs. Hazelton was standing.

"Yes, ma'am?"

"Come," she said as she disappeared back into the study.

"We need to talk before I go," Toni said.

"Go? What do you mean, go?"

She shook her head. "You need to talk to Mrs. Hazelton first."

She squeezed me tightly, gave me a kiss on the cheek and then released me and walked away.

Again I had to fight the urge to run after her. Partly I wanted to provide comfort to my best friend, my sister, and partly I wanted to avoid entering that room. Whatever had been said to her had reduced her to tears, and she was so much stronger than me.

As long as I didn't enter the study, whatever was waiting for me would have to keep waiting. It couldn't touch me or harm me as long as I stood right here. Once I stepped into the study, everything would change, and I'd be more alone than I'd ever been in my entire life.

"Betty," Mrs. Hazleton called out again.

"Coming, ma'am." I stumbled forward, the momentum of my body dragging my feet along. I stopped just inside the doorway. Mrs. Hazelton was seated behind her desk.

"Close the door and have a seat."

I closed the door and eased into the soft leather armchair that sat across from the desk. Some of the girls hated coming in here. Private discussions with the door closed often meant you were in trouble or about to be punished. I'd never really been in trouble or needed to be punished. This was simply a place I'd come to borrow a book from the shelves or have a cup of tea and a quiet conversation with Mrs. Hazelton. I knew that underneath that formal public face, she was gentle and kind. Some of my favorite memories were of things that had taken place inside this room. This morning was going to be different.

"Were you able to get any sleep, my dear?" she asked.

"A few moments," I said.

We had slept in the church down the road, each girl taking a pew as a bed. The few times I closed my eyes, I could only see the images of our house burning to the ground, leaving only ash and metal and a few smoldering, blackened wooden beams poking into the sky.

By the time the firemen had run a hose up from the pond, it was too late. With nobody inside to save and no chance of saving the building, there was no point to them risking their lives. They watched as the house burned to the ground.

The fire had moved surprisingly quickly. One of the firemen mentioned something about dry wood, that the whole building was nothing more than kindling. In the end, it wasn't even that. For the firemen, it was a fire. For us, it was the destruction of our home, the end of everything we'd ever known.

At the end of the night Mrs. Hazelton had collapsed. We all knew she hadn't been well for months, and the strain finally overcame her. Even then, she hadn't let the firemen and the doctor bring her back to her cottage until she was certain we were all tended to. Most of the little girls had been herded into cars and taken away to stay with local families, but I'd stayed much longer, watching. I figured the more I saw, the more real it would become. But it never became real.

"And ma'am, how are you feeling this morning?" I asked.

"I am doing as well as possible under the circumstances. Thank you for asking."

Mrs. Hazelton started to give more details about the aftermath of the fire. I listened but also studied her closely to see how she was *really* doing. She looked fine but faded, a grayer and paler shade of her normal self. But what else could be expected? *Stoic* was the word that best described her. No matter what, head up, emotions in check, moving forward. Lead by example. Even if she was on the verge of dying, I didn't think we'd see it. Was she on the verge? Her sickness wasn't a topic for discussion.

"Your clothes seem to fit you fairly well," Mrs. Hazelton said.

"Yes, ma'am."

"Perhaps not the most stylish clothing," she added. I remained silent. "The townsfolk were so generous in answering our call for clothes."

Starting at first light, people had rolled up in their cars and dropped off bags of clothing, footwear and personal items like toothbrushes. We had all lost everything we owned except for the nightgowns we'd worn to bed. The only exception was Tess, who had the clothes she'd been wearing. Everything else was gone. Clothing, shoes, books, stuffed animals, trinkets, inexpensive jewelry and little tokens that meant nothing to anyone else but everything to the girl who owned them. Now all I owned was the worn clothing on my back, a change of clothes in a donated suitcase and the ill-fitting shoes on my feet. All of it was used except for some undergarments that had been donated by a shop in town. I had virtually nothing and no place to go, which made having nothing even worse.

"I'll be helping the littler girls settle into their temporary homes," Mrs. Hazelton said.

"I'm sure that will be most comforting to them."

"Small comfort, but the best I can do," she said. She looked as sad as I felt.

"I know you'll do the best that can be done for them. For all of us," I said.

Her look of sadness became even deeper.

"I've always enjoyed our conversations in this room," she said. A small, sad smile crept over her face.

"I have too."

"You have both an inquiring mind and a positive outlook. Your optimism has been a blessing to us all. Betty, you know that I care for all of my girls. You are all special to me; you are my children," she said. "You all have your gifts. In you, there is an extraordinary kindness. You always seem to see the positive in everything and everybody."

"I try to, ma'am."

"I don't think I've ever heard you say a bad thing about another person in the almost fourteen years since you first arrived. It was just before your fourth birthday."

"I know, although I don't remember it. I don't remember anything from before or even that much from my first year or so here," I said. "This is all I've known."

And now it was gone. Not that it was going to last that much longer anyway. For me and the other six oldest girls, the plan had been that we would remain at the orphanage until we turned eighteen and then we'd be sent out into the world as independent adults. I was about to graduate from high school, and when I turned eighteen, I had planned to leave and work for a year or possibly two and then get further training. I wanted to become a nurse.

Even before the fire, there were changes coming to the orphanage. Some government people somewhere had decided that our orphanage—all orphanages—would be closed. The Home hadn't been accepting new residents for the past few years. Some of the younger girls had already been placed with foster families.

"I hoped that my illness would not prevent me from being here to oversee all the changes, to help my girls take the next step," Mrs. Hazelton said.

That mention of her illness caught me off guard. She hardly ever talked about it. She had been ill for the better part of a year but had only told us a few months ago. She hadn't told us what was wrong, just that she was *not well*. Over the past few months there had seemed to be less and less of her. She was withering away before our eyes, looking older and thinner every day. Even the way she walked, her posture slightly hunched, was telling, and there were times I was positive she was in pain. Not that she would ever tell us.

"I imagine this is a lesson in being careful what you wish for," Mrs. Hazelton said. "Here I am at the end."

"This isn't the end," I said.

She gave a weak smile. "Yes, I'm afraid it is." She paused again, as if struggling to find words. That was so unlike her. She had always known what to say.

"Betty, as you are aware, your eighteenth birthday marks your move into adulthood and independence. In a few months you were going take the job that I had arranged for you."

"Yes, ma'am."

"That was the plan. Man makes plans and God laughs. Last night He laughed. Our schedule has had to be moved forward."

"How much forward?"

"You'll be leaving today."

"I'm leaving today?" I gasped, unable to believe my ears.

"This afternoon."

I felt as if I'd been kicked in the stomach.

"I made a telephone call early this morning, and the employer has very graciously agreed to accommodate you immediately. There is no place for you here, and there is a place for you there."

"But what about school?"

"I know it means that you won't be able to finish your year, and it might interfere with your graduation."

"But it's only a few weeks until I'm finished."

"The timing is so unfortunate. I am going to try to make arrangements to allow you to graduate."

"Thank you," I stammered. What else could I say?

"I can only imagine how difficult this must be for you. Some of the girls were counting the days until they were old enough to leave. You've never been that way."

"I'd stay here forever if I could."

"Nothing is forever. It's important to remember that this isn't a new plan—it's all just happening earlier than expected. Nothing we can do about it, so there's no sense crying over spilled milk."

I bit down on the inside of my cheek. I was close to tears.

"You'll be going to a good home. The work is not glamorous, but it is honest work and fine training to someday become a wife and a mother," she said.

"Yes, ma'am."

"I know others may have greater plans, but I'm grounded in my own time. Lord knows it's 1964 and some people want to erase the roles we have played in the past, but I firmly believe a woman's place is in the home, and her role is to be a supportive wife and loving mother. Someday you will be a wonderful mother."

"I can only hope."

"A tragedy took away your family, but that tragedy cannot take away the opportunity to create your own family."

"I've always thought this was my family, this was my home," I said.

"It was...but it's all gone. You'll have time to say goodbye to the others. Your train leaves at 3:30 PM."

"My train?"

"Yes, you'll be going to Kingston by train," she said. "The future has arrived, Betty. And so has your past. You're returning to where you were born."

"I was born in Kingston?"

"There's so much you're not supposed to know. Some things are better forgotten, better left unknown. Some things, though, need to be known, even if it's not right."

I suddenly felt afraid. It wasn't so much her words as the tone of her voice and a darkness that seemed to cloud her eyes.

"Betty, did you ever wonder why you were never adopted?"

"I guess God didn't find the right family for me."

This was something Mrs. Hazelton had never talked about. *Nobody* ever talked about this. It was too painful.

For some reason, I'd been unwanted by my own family, but also by any other family.

"You know it's harder with older children, and while four doesn't seem old, everybody wants a baby. But then, when there was a couple or two that were interested, I had to talk to them, tell them something about your past."

"My past?"

"You must be curious. It's only natural to want to know. You must have questions."

I nodded my head ever so slightly. I did want to know, but I was afraid of what I might find out. Learning could never be unlearned.

"There are so many rules. When we discharge a ward at eighteen, we're only allowed to give minor details—what they call *nonidentifiable information*. This is general information that doesn't include anything that would allow you to know or locate your birth parents. Today I'm going to break those rules." She paused. "Sometimes you have to look back in order to move forward."

She picked up a large manila envelope that was on her desk and started to remove some papers. Then she hesitated. She looked at me and I could see the doubt in her eyes, the tears that were starting to form. I'd never seen her cry.

I reached across the table and placed my hand on hers. "I want to know. I can handle it."

Three

JOE COAXED THE beat-up old truck along the road. The engine sputtered and wheezed. For the past few months I'd wondered if the truck was going to last much longer. It turned out it was lasting longer than the orphanage. Longer than me. It would still be here when I was gone. He brought it to a stop at the intersection, and the engine stalled. Joe muttered something under his breath.

He turned the key and pumped the gas; the engine whined and spun and finally caught. A puff of blue smoke shot out from the exhaust pipe and drifted back into the window before he put the pickup in gear and started off again, leaving the haze behind.

"We're going to make it on time, aren't we?" I asked.

"We'll make it if I have to push the truck the rest of the way." Joe chuckled.

Part of me wanted us not to make it. If we missed the train I could go back with Joe. Sleeping in the church wasn't the same as sleeping in my room, but at least I'd still be with the girls for another night. At least, some of the girls. Toni had already gone—without saying goodbye. Not to anybody. Not even to me. How could she do that? I was her best friend in the world, and she'd just gone.

"Kingston's a fine place," Joe said.

"That's what Mrs. Hazelton said. I was born there."

"Do say."

"Not that I remember it. It's where my mother lived before my father..." I let the sentence trail off. I didn't know how much Joe knew, but I just didn't want to say the words. Saying them would make them even more true. "You were born in the south, right?"

"Louisiana, born and raised." He paused. "'Course, I don't have no accent anymore." He flashed a big smile, and that made me smile back and, for an instant, feel warmer inside. "Kingston is nice. Of course, it's no Toronto," Joe said. "That's where I'm headed."

"You're not staying here in Hope?"

"I'll be here for a while, helping with the cleanup and wrapping things up, but I'm definitely heading to Toronto once that's done, 'cause there won't be nothing else for me here anymore."

I suddenly felt bad. His room had been a small space off the kitchen, gone the same way our rooms had gone.

And with no orphans and no orphanage, there certainly wasn't a need for a cook.

"I'm so sorry. In all the rush and worrying about everything, I hadn't even thought about what would happen to you."

"No need to apologize or worry. This here cat has nine lives, and I think there are at least two of them left."

"What are you going to do in Toronto?" I asked.

"I was thinkin' that maybe it's time for me to pick up my guitar again."

"You plan to play the guitar for money?"

"We all knew the orphanage was goin' to close, so I've been making plans. I still know a few people, although not as many as I used to. Lots of them are dead or in jail, but I think I can hook myself up with a band, play a few gigs, get a little work."

"That would be wonderful. You're such a good player."

"I figure I'm the best player in Hope. 'Course, there's not a lot of competition."

"If there were a hundred players, you'd still be the best," I said.

"Kind of you to say so."

"I mean it."

"I know you do. 'Sides, if I can't get any gigs, I can live off my savings for a while. Then, if worse comes to worst, I can sure enough get work in a kitchen. I do have twenty-two years of experience, and a cook is a cook. People always need to eat." He paused. "It will also be good to be around some of my own people again."

"People from the south, from Louisiana?"

He laughed. "No, musicians. We're all just one big family. Don't matter if a man is from the north or south, whether he's old or young, whether he's white or a Negro. The music makes us all brothers."

I guess I understood that. The girls at the orphanage were sisters even though we had different mothers and fathers. We were all close—so why hadn't Toni said goodbye?

"I know you're sad about Toni leaving the way she did," Joe said.

I startled out of my thoughts. How did he know I was thinking about her?

"She didn't have much choice. She chased herself away. I think because the two of you were so close, she didn't know how to say goodbye," he said.

Were so close? I thought. If we really were so close, she would have found the time, found a way. Then again, in my rush to get out, I hadn't offered more than a few words and hugs to the others. I'd kept telling myself it was just goodbye for now. I had to think the same thing about Toni. I had to. It was the only way to move forward.

"That's not the last you'll see of each other," Joe said. "Toni said she'd write. You're all supposed to write."

"We're to send our letters to Mrs. Clifford at Loretta's Diner, and she will forward them once she has our new addresses," I said.

"That's a good plan. I'll make sure to drop a line or two myself, in case you girls are interested in what happens to old Joe."

"We'd be very interested—or I know I would be. Please write!"

"I will. You know, when I came to be a cook at the orphanage I figured it was only gonna be for a month or two tops. I'd save me a little money and be gone."

"But you've been there since before I arrived," I said.

"A week became a month and a month became a year and then a year sure enough became twenty-two years." He paused. "Do you know what happened?"

I shook my head.

"I got comfortable, and, maybe more than that, I got happy. I'd drifted halfway around the world and never felt like I had a home. At the orphanage, I got treated like I belonged."

"You do belong—I mean, you *did* belong. You were part of our family."

"And you were all part of mine." He laughed. "Who would have thunk that I'd have two dozen daughters?"

His laughter, as always, was infectious, and despite my fears I found myself laughing along.

"'Sides, I always liked cooking, and it wasn't like I didn't still have my music."

He'd had his guitar, and that little transistor in his room, which he'd brought to the kitchen when he worked. It was always on Top 40 hits throughout the day. At night, when he could get stations from far away, he'd listen to what he called Negro music. We could hear it through the walls of his room when we passed through the dining hall. He'd have it playing loud, and we could often hear him singing along to it. Some of it I liked, and some of it I wasn't sure of.

I knew Mrs. Hazelton didn't like it at all, and out of respect he'd turn it off when she was around. Her musical tastes pretty well ranged from anything classical to hymns. And, to be fair, Joe did help us with choir practice, and he did know all the old-time gospel and church songs as well as the songs on his transistor.

"I'm gonna really miss Toni," he said, "and I'm gonna miss you."

"I'm going to miss everybody, everything."

"I know you are, but you have to remember that you're gonna do just fine," he said. "It's Miss Toni that I'm most worried about."

That only made sense. He was closer to her than anybody else. They'd spent time together listening to and talking about music—and life.

"Not that I won't worry about all of you, but Miss Toni… she just isn't as tough as she thinks she is."

That surprised me. She was the strongest person I knew—well, except for Mrs. Hazelton.

"It's funny how Miss Toni went on about how she's always been worried about you, but she doesn't have to. All these years she's been thinkin' that she's the one looking after you."

"What do you mean?"

"Toni thinks she's so hard and you're so soft," Joe said. "I knows it's the other way around. You're the tough one."

"I'm not tough."

He put his foot on the brake, and I put my hand on the dashboard to stop myself from sliding off the seat. We came to a stop, right there on the road. What was happening? Had the truck stalled? No, the engine was still going.

He turned to face me. "Don't ever sell yourself short, and don't allow anybody else to do it either. You're a lot stronger than you think you are. Being kind doesn't mean being weak. Thinking the best of people doesn't mean you should think any less of yourself. Understand?"

I nodded my head, even though I didn't really understand or necessarily agree. Toni was the strong one, not me.

"You're not very big," he said.

"I know." I was so small that most people thought I was a year or two younger than I was.

"And because you're almost always smiling, some people mistake small and friendly for weak. You have to use those things to your advantage," Joe said.

"I don't know what you mean."

"Let 'em underestimate you. Let 'em think there's no steel beneath the surface. You have lots of people fooled that way."

"I'm not trying to fool anybody."

"Didn't say you were trying. It just happens. They see the smile instead of the steel underneath it. You, Miss Betty, are a survivor."

A horn honked, and we both turned around. A car had come up behind us. Joe waved at the other driver and put the truck back in gear, and we lurched forward. We continued until we reached the heart of the town and turned onto the main street of Hope. We drove by the Orpheus, where a lineup of people waited to go in for the matinee. I wasn't interested in the movie that was playing now, but Toni and I had made plans to go and see the next release—*Mary Poppins*. That wasn't going to happen now.

The parking lot of the grocery store was full, and there were people loading groceries into their cars. Mulcaster's front windows had mannequins displaying the newest clothes—all of which were far nicer than the cast-offs I was wearing. Walking along the streets were people I knew. They didn't notice us driving by. They couldn't know this would be the last time they'd see me, at least for a long, long time.

I looked at each little store as we passed. I knew them all. They were all that I *did* know. The pharmacy, the little clothing store where all I could do was window-shop, the variety store, the hardware store. I silently said goodbye to all of them, even the ones I'd never been inside.

We came out the other side of the downtown, stores giving way to houses, and then crossed over the railway tracks. They curved around, separating the town proper from the lake to the south, two silver slivers that mostly carried freight cars. A few times a day, a shiny passenger train briefly stopped as it made its way between Toronto and Montreal. I'd seen it many times but never thought I'd be getting on it—had never wanted to get on it. I still didn't.

Joe eased the truck into a spot in the parking lot. It wasn't crowded, but there were cars—and people—nearby. We climbed out and he grabbed my bag from the back.

"Traveling light is the way to go," he said as he handed me my bag.

"I guess none of us has much choice."

My suitcase was old and worn; one of the clasps didn't fasten properly. I supposed beggars couldn't be choosers. In the suitcase I had a change of clothing, an extra pair of shoes, a few personal items and, of course, my nightgown, the only thing that actually did belong to me.

In my purse—which, of course, had also been donated— was the envelope from Mrs. Hazelton, my ticket, a letter of introduction to my employer and the money Mrs. Hazelton had given me. I knew they were all in there because I'd doubled-checked and then checked again before we left. I pressed the purse tightly to my chest. It was like a shield against the world, its contents the only things that would offer me any protection.

As we walked to the station, there were very few people who didn't nod or say hello or acknowledge us in one way or another, and we answered back. Hope was so small that we either knew somebody or knew of them. There couldn't be a soul in town who didn't know about the fire.

I felt a little self-conscious and struggled to make polite eye contact. At times it had been hard enough that they all knew I was an orphan, but now it was even worse. I was an orphan without an orphanage, dressed in donated clothing, leaving town. I had always been an unwanted, homeless child, and now I was even more unwanted and homeless, no longer a child but still not an adult. If Joe was right and there was steel inside of me, I didn't feel it. Unless that cold feeling was the steel pressed against my bones. I was uneasy, even scared. I wished Toni were there with me.

"Looks like some joker has gotten to the sign again," Joe said.

Hanging from the side of the station was a big sign that said *HOPE*; in smaller letters someone had added *less*. I'd seen the town sign change many times—*No Hope, Small Hope, False Hope* and now *Hopeless*. Suddenly I felt all of those things. I clutched my purse even tighter.

Joe looked at his watch. "Won't be more than a few minutes before it arrives."

I was prepared to wait forever. Sometimes the train was late. I'd heard that sometimes it didn't even come at all.

"I guess I better be getting back," Joe said.

"You're going?" I exclaimed.

"I've never been much for goodbyes. Maybe that's why I didn't leave the orphanage before this. Besides, you won't have to wait for long."

"I was just hoping that...I'll be fine. Thank you for driving me."

Joe held out his hand to shake goodbye. I reached up and threw my arms around his neck, hugging him with all my might, almost pulling him off his feet. When I released my grip, Joe looked embarrassed.

"I'm going to miss you so much," I said.

"Me too."

"Goodbye, Jumpin' Joe," I said, calling him by his nickname.

I thought I saw a tear in the corner of his eye, but he turned away before I could tell for sure. I watched as he walked along the platform, moving past the other people, and then disappeared around the side of the station. He was gone. I had to fight the urge to run after him, jump in the truck and beg him to take me with him. A train horn sounded, and then the bells at the crossing started to chime. It was coming.

Within seconds I heard the sound of the train itself, although, looking down the track, I still couldn't see it around the curve of the rails. The drone of the engine got louder and louder, echoing off the station itself. Finally it rounded the curve, its bright front light leading the way. The engine got louder, and then I heard the squeal of metal wheels on metal tracks as the train started to brake. The front light was blindingly bright, causing me to look away. The sound of the engine got louder and louder, over-whelming me as the train entered the station, and I stepped back from the platform, partially propelled by the air that the train pushed before it.

It had hardly come to a stop when the doors opened and two conductors jumped off. Almost instantly, passengers followed. They were greeted with handshakes and hugs by the people waiting for them. All along the platform, other people were saying their last goodbyes. Hugs were often accompanied by tears.

I was so alone. Nobody was here to shed a tear when I left. I'd said my goodbyes to everybody, and now there was nobody here to see me off. There was nobody and nothing for me here. It was time to leave. I opened my purse, pulled out the ticket Joe had bought earlier in the day and walked over to one of the conductors. I handed him my ticket.

"Kingston," he said. He punched the ticket and handed it back to me.

"Thank you."

"Do you need help with your baggage?"

"No, thank you. This is all I have."

He offered me his hand to help me up the steps, and I entered the car. I saw a pair of empty seats and settled into the seat by the window, tucking my suitcase underneath me.

I looked out at the passengers being greeted with joy. Nobody would be on the Kingston platform to greet me that way. Nobody had been here at the end to say goodbye to me—not Toni, not Mrs. Hazelton, not even Joe.

The conductor blew his whistle and climbed back onto the train, disappearing from my view. The train clunked and started to move forward. And then I saw him—Joe, standing at the end of the platform. He had a smile on his face. I caught his eye, and he gave a big wave. I waved back and laughed, and he laughed too. As the train picked up speed, we passed him, leaving the platform behind. I went to spin around, to catch one last glimpse, but I stopped myself.

I wasn't going to struggle to hold on to what was gone. Who knew when or under what circumstances I might see Joe or Toni or Mrs. Hazelton? It could be in a few months or in a few years or longer. It could be by myself or with a husband—perhaps even with children. I could be on this same train or looking through the windshield of a bus or even in a fine car driven by my husband. I didn't know anything for certain, but I knew it would be good, and I wouldn't be wearing another woman's clothes.

Right now I needed to look forward, into my future. But before I could do that, I needed to look deeper into my past.

Four

I NIBBLED ON the sandwich Joe had made for me. The last thing he'd ever make for me. The last piece of home. I saved one little corner. It wasn't just that I might be hungry later, but also that as long as I had that little slice, I still had something from home. I rewrapped it in its wax paper and put it back into my purse, nestled in beside the brown envelope—*the* envelope. It stared up as if it had eyes and breath and life. Well, it did have one life—mine—inside it.

I'd now exhausted all the possible excuses I'd put in the way of what I had to do. I'd eaten, looked out the window, even tried unsuccessfully to sleep and then, equally unsuccessfully, to write a letter to Toni. Now there was nothing left in the way. I didn't know why I was still so afraid of it. It wasn't as if it contained anything I already didn't know about.

I looked all around, as if ashamed to have somebody see me look in the envelope, as if any of my few fellow passengers knew what it contained.

Slowly I removed the envelope from my purse. I let it sit on my lap, my fingers running along the edge. Once more I glanced around. An older woman seated across the aisle gave me a small smile, which I returned.

"Beautiful view," the woman said. I was a little startled.

"Yes, it is, ma'am."

"Where are you off to?"

"Kingston."

"I'm visiting my daughter and my grandchildren in Montreal," she said. "What takes you to Kingston?"

"I'm going for work."

She looked confused. "You don't seem old enough to work."

"I'm older than I look."

"Unfortunately, I'm as old as I look." She laughed, and I laughed along. It felt good.

"My daughter and her husband just moved to Montreal. It's where I was born."

"I was born in Kingston," I said.

It was strange to hear those words out loud. I'd never said them to anybody except Joe. Until earlier today, I hadn't known where I was born. I'd just assumed it was right around Hope. It would have been better if I'd known all along. I wouldn't have wondered if my mother was somebody I passed in the streets of Hope. And I would have known there was no way I was ever going to see her anywhere.

"Kingston is a lovely town," she said. "I'm sure you'll be very happy there."

"I'm sure I will."

I offered the woman another little smile and glanced down at the envelope. My last excuse was gone, and now my uneasy feelings came to the surface. This was silly. It wasn't like I didn't know what was in there. I'd already looked at each slip of paper, read them over a few times, but still, it was so unreal. I hoped by reading them again they'd become more real. In this envelope was my history, my background. Maybe looking back was the way forward—that's what Mrs. Hazelton had said—but how could any of this information help me move anywhere?

I started with the smallest piece of paper. It was tattered and faded blue.

Certificate of Birth

Name: Elizabeth Anne Roberts

Date of Birth: Dec. 24, 1946

Sex: F

Place of Birth: Kingston, Ontario

Registration: Jan. 14, 1947

I ran my fingers along the words and numbers. There weren't many, but they were everything I needed to know, everything I *was*.

Elizabeth Anne Roberts. I'd always liked the name Elizabeth—it was regal. *Queen* Elizabeth. How much more regal could you be than the Queen of England? But it wasn't me. I was just Betty, plain Betty, Betty Shirley, the person I'd been my entire life. Well, not exactly my whole life, but the life I'd known since I was almost four, since I'd come to live at the orphanage, since the time that...I turned to the next two papers.

They were large, faded, yellow with age and delicate to the touch. They had been clipped from the front page of the *Kingston Whig-Standard* newspaper. The first was dated September 11, 1950. The headline was right below the title of the paper. In big bold capital letters, the words practically jumped off the page.

MURDER IN KINGSTON

I read the headline two more times before I read the text, somehow hoping that this time it would say something different.

KINGSTON—Police officers responding to a routine domestic assault in a house in the Inner Harbour District were shocked to discover the body of Kingston resident Victoria Roberts. Along with the body they discovered the woman's three-year-old daughter, covered in her mother's blood and clinging to her mother, who had suffered obvious head wounds. The grisly discovery was made in the backyard of the house where the victim resided with her daughter, at the corner of Charles and Montreal. Ambulance services were also dispatched, but Miss Roberts was declared dead on the scene.

A twenty-year-old unmarried mother, Miss Roberts was a long-time Kingston resident who had no known relatives, her parents having predeceased her in a car accident.

Police report that there have been previous calls to this address for similar reasons, and an officer reported that he felt it was "just a matter of time until something happens." The police are seeking a person of interest, Mr. Gordon Sullivan, the boyfriend of the victim. He is described as standing in excess of six feet three inches and weighing over 250 pounds and is well known to the police. Anyone knowing of his whereabouts is requested to contact the police and not to approach, as he is considered dangerous.

The child, Elizabeth Anne, suffered no injuries. The investigating detectives and a matron from social services who interviewed the girl believe she did not actually witness the murder of her mother. She has been taken into protective services awaiting further exploration to find suitable family members.

The report continued on another page—a page that wasn't included in my package.

No matter how many times I read the article, it didn't seem real. I felt so sad for that poor child and had to remind myself that *I* was that poor child. I was Elizabeth Anne—that was who I was. I was that little girl, almost four years old, who had clung to the body of her mother in the backyard of her house. I couldn't remember the house.

I couldn't remember my mother. I couldn't remember the scene. If it wasn't for the birth certificate, if it wasn't for Mrs. Hazelton swearing that it was me, I wouldn't have believed it.

There was one other newspaper clipping, taken from the front page of the same paper three months later. The headline was equally bold and just as troubling.

MAN CONVICTED OF MURDER

I started to read it again but skipped over the first few paragraphs. I'd gone over it a dozen times as well and didn't need to know anything more about the trial. I scanned down the page.

> Mr. Sullivan, the on-again, off-again boyfriend of the victim, Miss Victoria Roberts, is also the father of the child, Elizabeth Anne Roberts, age three. In a fit of rage and passion, Mr. Sullivan—who has previous convictions for assault—took the life of Miss Roberts and robbed young Elizabeth Anne of both her mother and her father.
>
> Throughout the trial, Mr. Sullivan maintained his innocence, even taking the stand in his own defense and pleading his innocence to the jury. The presiding judge, the Honorable Mr. Justice Stern, said that while the witness was highly credible in arguing his innocence, under cross-examination Mr. Sullivan was not

able to provide a suitable explanation for why the murder weapon—a hammer—was found hidden in a closet in his residence. Mr. Sullivan claimed that he was "framed" but was unable to provide either an explanation of who might have done this or names of any other possible suspects who would have had motive to take Miss Roberts's life.

In addressing the court and jury after hearing the guilty verdict, Mr. Sullivan again maintained his innocence and offered the jury his "forgiveness" for convicting an innocent man and depriving his daughter of the care of her remaining parent.

I felt like my heart had turned to stone. That was me. I was the daughter.

In handing down his sentence, Justice Stern indicated that he felt the murder was a "crime of passion" and not premeditated. He therefore endorsed a verdict of second-degree murder, sparing Mr. Sullivan from the death penalty. However, due to the "cowardly" nature of the attack and the unwillingness of the accused to accept responsibility, the judge sentenced him to the maximum allowable time—25 years— with a strong recommendation that he not be eligible for parole and instead serve his entire sentence.

I felt my breath catch in my throat, and tears started to come to my eyes. I brushed them away with the back of my hand. I went to put the clipping down on my lap and then thought better of it. I put it back in the envelope, out of sight.

Growing up, I'd had the same two dreams, the same two fantasies, that every other orphan—at least, the ones I knew—seemed to have: that someday I'd be adopted, or that one day my *real* mother would walk in and take me away. The two fantasies would ebb and flow, fade and grow. As one got stronger, the other faded.

When I was young, there were always thoughts, whispers, in the back of my head: today could be the day I'd become part of a family. The thoughts were still there when I went to bed at night, and I'd offer them as a prayer. I remembered lying in bed, whispering with Toni in the dark about the families we dreamed about. How we thought it was only going to be a matter of time until it happened. After all, some of the children got adopted. We ignored the fact that they were almost always babies or at least kids who were much younger than we were.

Some of our discussions were about the house we'd live in with our new families. Maybe we wouldn't have to share a room, maybe we'd have more clothing—*new* clothing—or even a dog. It was our dream to become part of a family, to belong somewhere, to finally be wanted by somebody, even if we hadn't been wanted by our mothers or fathers.

Sometimes Toni and I talked about one family adopting the two of us. Even if the family only wanted one child, we'd say they had to take us both or they couldn't have either of us. I don't know if Toni really would have gone through with it—or if I would have either—but it made us feel better. Not only would we have parents and a home, but also we'd be sisters. But would a true sister have gone away without saying goodbye? I couldn't let myself think like that. Even if I couldn't hold on to Toni, I needed to hang on to the memory of our friendship. After all, what else did I have?

My second fantasy was just as strong. Someday the door would open and, instead of an adoptive parent, my real mother or father would walk in, claim me and take me back to my real family and real home. And there would have been a *really good* reason why they had given me up. I'd be reunited with my brothers and sisters, and our house would be beautiful, and my mother would be ever so kind.

Maybe my mother was royalty and there had been a plot against the throne. To protect me, my parents had sent me away, and now the situation had been resolved. I'd forgive them and we'd all live happily ever after.

As we got older the fantasies and dreams came less often, because the reality became stronger. There was only going to be ebb and no flow, fade and no grow. I didn't remember when the fantasies stopped completely, but they did. Nobody was going to adopt me and nobody was going to rescue me. I came to accept that. Still, in some little corner of my mind, there had been a little slice of hope.

Until I read those articles.

My mother was dead. She wasn't coming back. I'd never pass her on the street, not knowing who she was. We'd never meet by chance and discover our connection; we'd never embrace and live our futures intertwined. We'd share no past and have no future. Now, finally, that last glimmer of hope had been taken away, killed this very day when I found out that my mother had been killed—had been murdered.

I felt confused. I needed to think. No, I needed *not* to think. I needed to sleep. I shut my eyes tightly and placed a hand against them to block out the light. I'd try to sleep. I just hoped I wouldn't dream.

Five

MY EYES POPPED open. There was a hand on my shoulder and a woman standing over me.

"Dear, isn't this your stop?" she asked. "This is Kingston."

Then it came back. I was on a train and—

"You are getting off in Kingston, aren't you?"

I jumped up, and my purse and the papers on my lap scattered and dropped to the floor. I reached down and gathered them up, crumpling them and stuffing them into my purse. I was partway down the aisle when I realized I'd forgotten my bag under the seat. I raced back and tried to pull it free, but it was jammed. I gave an extra-hard tug, and it popped free, causing me to almost tumble over backward.

"Thank you, thank you so much," I called to the woman.

"Hurry, dear. The train is about to leave."

Bag in one hand, purse in the other, I ran down the aisle toward a door. I got there just in time to see the conductor at the bottom of the stairs with the little step stool in his hands.

"Please wait, I have to get off!"

"Cutting it a little close," he said as he offered me a hand.

"I'm sorry—I fell asleep. Thank you."

No sooner had my feet hit the platform than he and his stool jumped back on board and he leaned out and waved for the engineer to start the train.

I turned and looked back along the tracks. Somewhere back there was the life I'd known. I had the strangest thought—I could just turn around and walk back. It would take days, of course, but it couldn't be much more than a hundred miles, and if I walked for a few days I could...I let it go. It was the silly thought of a scared little girl. I was scared, but I wasn't a little girl. I was strong. That's what Joe had said. I had to face the present. My life, whatever it would become, was right here. Besides, I had other, more pressing things to think about. Rather than entertaining any thoughts of walking back to Hope, I had to get myself to my new home and my new place of employment.

The platform was now empty. I was alone. I walked over to the station, took a seat on the bench, placed my suitcase at my feet and pulled out my purse. Carefully I removed my birth certificate and the newspaper clippings and smoothed them out. One of the clippings had ripped, and the headline MAN CONVICTED OF MURDER was split in two. I folded the papers together and slid them back into my purse, this time more carefully. Somewhere in my purse was the address I needed. Mrs. Hazelton had said my new home wasn't too far from the station. I could ask the station master for directions and walk.

I fumbled around in my purse, but I couldn't find the slip of paper with the address on it. What if it had fallen out of my purse when I dropped it on the train? What would I do then? It wasn't as if I'd memorized the address or—there the paper was, tucked away in the bottom of my purse. I pulled it out, unfolded it and read it: 1121 Sydenham Street.

I let out a sigh of relief. Now that I knew where I was going, all I had to do was get there. If I'd fantasized about walking back to Hope, I could certainly stroll across Kingston. Kingston was bigger than Hope by a long shot, but it wasn't so big that I couldn't walk from one side of it to the other if I had to.

"Are you Betty?"

I looked up. A man in a black suit stood over me.

"Are you Betty?" he asked again.

I hesitated for a split second and then replied, "My name is Elizabeth Anne."

"Sorry to bother you," he said. "I'm here to pick up somebody named Betty Shirley."

He was half a step away before I called out, "Wait!" and jumped to my feet. "My friends call me Betty."

He looked suspicious, as if I was lying to him to get a ride.

"I'm here to take up a position at the Remington residence," I explained.

His expression resolved into a smile, and he nodded his head. "Then you're the person I'm here to get."

"Are you Mr. Remington?"

He burst into laughter, which caught me by surprise. I felt embarrassed.

"I'm James, the Remingtons' *driver*."

I held out my hand. "I'm very pleased to meet you, sir."

"No need to call me sir," he said as we shook. "Here, let me take your bag."

Before I could object, he swept down and picked it up, turning on his heels and heading away. I scrambled after him.

"It was nice of you to come and get me," I said.

"Just following orders."

"Mr. Remington sent you?"

"Mr. Remington has been gone and buried for a good twenty-five years."

"I'm sorry to hear that."

"Why, did you know him?" he asked.

"Of course not! I wasn't even born twenty-five years ago. It's just that it's sad that he passed on," I said.

"If you'd known the man, you would know it wasn't that sad a day."

I didn't know what to say or how to react.

He stopped beside a large black car—the fanciest car I'd ever seen in my entire life. He opened up the trunk, placed my suitcase in it and then walked to the side and opened up the front passenger door, gesturing for me to get in. I did.

He closed the door and circled around, getting in behind the wheel.

"This is a beautiful car," I said as he started the engine.

"It is not simply *a* beautiful car," James said. "It is *the* most beautiful car. This is a 1961 Rolls-Royce Silver Cloud."

"I've never even seen one of these before."

"Not surprising, as there are no more than a handful in the entire country, and this is the only one I know of between Montreal and Toronto."

"It's just beautiful." I ran my hand along the wooden dashboard.

"Walnut. The best of the best in everything is almost the Remington family motto." He put the car in gear and we glided away. "It is the epitome of elegance, luxury and good breeding."

"I like the thing on the hood," I said, gesturing to the ornament at the end of the very, very long hood.

"She is referred to as the Spirit of Ecstasy, the Silver Lady or the Flying Lady."

"She's beautiful too."

"She should be, since she's worth more than many of the cars on the road. Those in the know simply refer to her as Emily."

That made me laugh. "Hello, Emily," I said and waved at her.

"You have a fine laugh," he said. "It reminds me of some-body...I'm not sure who...but it does seem familiar."

As we moved slowly down a main street, I noticed that people on the street and drivers in other cars turned to look.

"Obviously, you don't know anything about the family you'll be working for," James said.

I shook my head. "Nothing, nothing at all."

"The lady of the house is Mrs. Remington. You can refer to her as either Ma'am or Mrs. Remington. She is in her early seventies. Unlike her departed husband, who could politely be described as impolite, she is a true lady. She treats her staff with respect and dignity." He paused. "She is well liked and respected by all the staff."

"How many staff are there?"

"There is, of course, myself, and the gardener, a cook and the maid."

"I thought I was hired to be the maid."

"Believe me, there is enough house to need two maids," he said. "Besides, Mrs. Meyers is more the head of staff than simply the maid."

"But do you really need all of those people for one person?"

"The house is also home to her son, Richard Junior."

"How old is he?" I asked.

"Depends on how you mean that," he said.

How many ways *could* I mean that?

"He's got to be close to forty years old," James said, "but up here"—he tapped the side of his head—"he's a bit, shall we say, *special*."

An uneasy feeling came over me, and it must have shown.

"But don't worry about him. He's friendly enough and completely harmless. He spends most of his time in the backyard in the pigeon coop."

The car came to a stop in front of a large metal gate. Beyond the gate, beyond the long, lush lawn, was a big white house.

"Welcome home," James said.

Six

MRS. MEYERS LOOKED me up and down, and I dropped my eyes to the ground. She brushed her hands over my apron to smooth it out.

"It seems a bit big, my dear," she said with her strong Scottish burr.

"Yes, ma'am, a bit big."

"I'll take it in this evening, but for tonight it will have to do. I had no idea you'd be such a wee lass."

"Sorry, ma'am."

"Are you apologizing for being small?"

"No, I mean…sort of. I didn't mean to put you to any more work."

"Actually, you're going to save me a great deal of work," she said. "I must admit I was rather surprised when Mrs. Remington informed me that she was bringing on another servant, but many hands make light work."

"I'll work as hard as I can," I promised.

She looked at me with a thoughtful expression. Was she questioning what I'd said?

"You look familiar. Perhaps I've seen you around town."

"I just arrived on the train from Hope. I've never been here before…well, except when I was very young."

"Regardless, there's something about you," she said. "Do you see it, Nigel?"

She turned to the cook, who was standing over the stove.

He offered a shrug. "All maids look the same to me. I can hardly tell the two of you apart."

Mrs. Meyers chuckled. "I'll take that as a compliment. It's been almost forty years since I've seen her side of twenty. How old are you, child?"

"Almost eighteen."

"I was younger than you when I started working for the family."

"Really?"

"Is your response because you can't imagine that I've ever been young or that I've worked for the family that long?"

I was ready to stammer out another apology when both she and the cook started to laugh.

"Most of us have been here a long time," Mrs. Meyers said.

"I'm almost twenty years," Nigel said as he turned away from the stove to face us. "Actually, she does look familiar to me as well."

I shrugged. "I guess I just have that sort of face."

"No, you don't, but you do look familiar."

"Come on now, Elizabeth. We'll get the table set for dinner."

For a split second I didn't realize she was talking to me. I still wasn't sure why I'd introduced myself to first James and then to her as Elizabeth Anne, but I had. For better or for worse, I was in a new town and I had a new name. Or, really, an old name, my real name.

Mrs. Meyers handed me a tray filled with plates and cutlery. It was heavy, and I had to be firm in my grip. The last thing I wanted to do on my first day was break all these fine dishes.

I followed her out of the kitchen and up the stairs—the servants' stairs. They were steep and narrow and grooved from so much use, and I had to be careful where I stepped. At the top was a small landing, and she propped open a door that led directly into the dining room. I stopped and looked around in awe. It was gigantic—bigger than the dining area at the orphanage—with a high ceiling and dark, polished furniture. At the center of the room was a large table that had a dozen chairs tucked in around it.

"Quite impressive, isn't it?" Mrs. Meyers said.

"Very. I've never been in a place like this before."

"Tomorrow I'll take you for a tour of the entire house. It's one of the most elegant homes in all of Kingston. Place the tray on the sideboard," she ordered.

I set it down carefully, making sure not to scratch the wood. I was relieved to have delivered it safely. I could only suspect, but I thought the plates on the tray might be worth much more than my monthly wages.

"Watch what I do very carefully."

Mrs. Meyers set down plates, side plates, soup bowls, fine white napkins and a glistening array of cutlery. I didn't understand why each person needed so many forks and spoons. Next, she put down a fine crystal glass beside each place setting.

"There's an etiquette as to how a table should be set," she explained. "You'll pick it up quickly." She motioned for me to come closer, which I did. "This is Mrs. Remington's spot, and things have to be very precise," she whispered. "With her fading sight, it's even more important that each thing, especially the glass, is in *exactly* the correct spot." She nudged the glass over a touch.

"How bad are—"

Mrs. Meyers shushed me. "Her *hearing* is very good," she whispered. "And she doesn't like us talking about it. Her eyes…not so good and getting worse. Cataracts. Her eyes are all clouded over, poor dear, and then there's a degenerative condition, something that can't be fixed or cured."

She finished off the fourth place setting and went over to where we had entered the room, but I couldn't see a door. She put her hand against a wall panel, and it popped open to reveal the passage we'd come through.

"That's clever," I said.

"There are many disguised doors in this house," Mrs. Meyers said.

"It's like something from an old movie," I said as we started down the steep stairs.

"This house is full of little passages, hidden doors and rooms. Partly it's to keep the servants out of sight. A good servant should be neither heard nor seen, but simply be there when needed. Which reminds me, you are under no circumstances to speak unless you are spoken to. Understand?"

I nodded.

"I didn't mean with me. You can speak to me all you want. You're the new girl, by about fifteen years, but we're all pretty friendly. We consider ourselves a little family." She paused. "Speaking of which, where is your family?"

"I don't have a family."

"Everybody has a family."

I shook my head. "I was raised in an orphanage. The only family I have are the other girls—I call them my sisters—and now we're all scattered about, so, well, I don't have any family."

"You're wrong," Mrs. Meyers said firmly. "Starting today you do have a family—us. Right, Nigel?" she said as we entered the kitchen.

"Maybe not the best family in Kingston, but she's right. Just consider me that old uncle who never married and loves to cook."

"And I'm probably too old to be your mother, so think of me as your great-aunt," Mrs. Meyers said.

"Thank you, thank you so much," I said. I threw my arms around her, and judging from her expression, I caught her completely off guard. But there was nothing anybody could have said that would have made me feel better and less scared.

"There, there, dear," she said as she placed one arm around me and patted me on the back.

"If you two are finished hugging, the soup is ready to go upstairs," Nigel said.

I released my grip and Mrs. Meyers motioned for me to pick up the big soup tureen. The top was closed, but the steam and aroma still escaped. It was heavy. Just how much soup was in here?

Once again we started up the stairs. She pushed the panel open, and we entered the dining room again. The seats were still unoccupied.

"Place the soup over there," Mrs. Meyers said, pointing to the buffet.

I did as she asked. "That's a lot of soup for four people," I said.

"There won't be four people."

"Should we set out more places?" I asked.

She motioned for me to come closer. "There are four places set, but there are not going to be four people eating."

Now I was even more confused.

"Mrs. Remington always has us set four places. One for herself, a place for both of her sons and one for her husband."

"But I thought that her husband was…"

"He is. She has had us set a place for him at every meal every day since his death."

"That's touching."

"Some people might think it's a bit touched in the head," she said, her words barely a whisper.

"It's so nice that her sons are here to dine with her."

"It's rare that her youngest son, Edward, is here. He lives across town and either dines with his own family or is busy working. His *position* keeps him very occupied. Edward is the mayor of Kingston."

"I had no idea."

"He's been elected three times. He's a fine mayor and a *very* respected man."

"His mother must be proud of him. So it's just Mrs. Remington and her other son for dinner?"

She shook her head. "Richie most often eats on his own. We simply bring a meal out to the coop and he dines with his pigeons. It's most often Mrs. Remington and her music. Speaking of which, I should put on the music."

She disappeared around the corner, and music filled the room. I recognized it immediately. It was one of Mrs. Hazelton's favorite pieces.

Mrs. Meyers returned and almost immediately a second door opened and an old woman appeared. I slowly stepped back until I was pressed against the wall.

"Good evening, Mrs. Remington," Mrs. Meyers called out.

"Good evening, Edith."

Mrs. Meyers came over and held out a chair, and Mrs. Remington took a seat.

"The soup smells wonderful," she said.

"I'm sure it's as good as it smells."

Mrs. Meyers motioned to me. I took a soup bowl, placed it beside the tureen, removed the top and ladled in a serving of soup. Mrs. Meyers picked it up and placed it in front of Mrs. Remington.

"Will Master Edward be joining us this evening?" Mrs. Meyers asked.

"It appears not. His work has been keeping him rather busy over the past month."

"And Master Richard?"

"He seems to be even more occupied than the mayor. Did he even have any lunch today?"

"I had a plate sent out to him in his *office*," Mrs. Meyers said.

"That was very kind of you. Always taking care of my boys. I just wish you could have sent lunch over to Edward. You know his wife is a *dreadful* cook."

"I know her cook is quite capable, so there's no need for you to worry," Mrs. Meyers said.

"I think worrying is the only part of parenting that still applies to me."

"Yes, ma'am, no matter how old they are, or how old we are, we still worry about our babies," Mrs. Meyers said.

Had my mother worried about me? Was Mrs. Hazelton worried about me now? Not that she was my mother, but who else did I have?

"So it will only be Mr. Remington and me dining tonight."

"Yes, ma'am."

Mrs. Meyers motioned to me again, and I realized what she was asking. I lifted up the ladle and filled a second bowl with soup, which she promptly put down at the setting at the head of the table beside Mrs. Remington.

"Potato-leek soup was always one of my husband's favorites," Mrs. Remington said.

She put her hands together and closed her eyes. She was praying. Although I couldn't hear the words, I put my hands together, lowered my head, closed my eyes and said a silent prayer myself.

Dear God, thank you for the blessings in my life. Please keep me safe and give me the strength to go on, and protect me and my sisters and—

"Amen," Mrs. Remington said.

Amen, I said in my head and opened my eyes again.

"This soup is as wonderful as it smells!" Mrs. Remington said after she had tasted a spoonful. "Please pass on my compliments to Nigel."

"Certainly, ma'am. He'll be so pleased to hear that."

"So how was your day today, my dear?" Mrs. Remington asked.

I waited for Mrs. Meyers to answer, but she didn't say a word. She couldn't be talking to me, could she?

"Did you speak to our sons at all today?" she asked.

Then I realized it wasn't either of us she was talking to— it was her *husband.* She was having a conversation with the empty place setting beside her.

"Our newest staff member must think her employer is crazy," Mrs. Remington said.

I heard the words but didn't instantly understand they *were* for my ears. Mrs. Meyers gestured for me to answer.

"Yes, ma'am. I mean, no, ma'am."

"I know my dear husband isn't here, but somehow it keeps him nearer to my heart to have our conversations. Before my sight left me, I used to write him letters. Does that seem odd?"

"No, ma'am. I know what it's like not to be around the people you care for," I said. I thought about Toni and Mrs. Hazelton and all the other girls, my own little family that had been thrown to the winds, and for a split second I thought about the mother I never knew except for what I'd read in a newspaper clipping.

"You'd be surprised how talking to somebody who isn't with you can bring you closer. You should try it sometime," she said.

I didn't know about having a conversation, but I was going to write Toni a letter. I hoped she'd write back.

"Come closer, my dear. I don't bite, regardless of what Mrs. Meyers might have told you."

"She only had good things to tell me—honestly!"

"I'm just teasing. Mrs. Meyers is a dear friend and a kind soul—as I imagine you are too. Come closer."

Slowly, I moved until I was standing right beside her.

"I'd like you to sit down so we can talk and I can get to know you better," she said and gestured to the seat beside her.

I looked to Mrs. Meyers for guidance, and she nodded. That didn't relieve the shivers that were radiating throughout my body, but I did as I was told and sat down.

"What would you like to be called?" she asked. Her voice was gentle, and she was looking directly at me, although I didn't know how much she could really see.

"Elizabeth Anne," I said.

"Do your friends ever shorten it, perhaps call you Lizzy?" she asked.

"No, ma'am. My friends called me Betty."

"Not the usual short form of Elizabeth."

"Well, I wasn't really an Elizabeth. It's hard to explain."

She reached out a hand and placed it on top of one of mine. "I know exactly how complicated it is." She turned to face Mrs. Meyers. "My eyes don't allow me to see, but I can certainly hear something familiar in Elizabeth's voice. Do you hear it?"

"I can't really say I can, but both Nigel and I thought that she looked familiar."

I sat there feeling more and more uncomfortable.

"I can hear it with my own ears, so I know it's true," Mrs. Remington said. "I can hear her in Elizabeth's voice the way you can see her with your eyes."

This was getting even more uncomfortable, and confusing, and I was feeling anxious.

"This is little Lizzy," Mrs. Remington said.

Mrs. Meyers's expression mirrored my confusion.

"I don't understand," I said.

"Lizzy. Our Lizzy. The little girl who lived in this house," Mrs. Remington said.

"This is Lizzy?" Mrs. Meyers questioned. "It can't be... can it?"

"You said it yourself—she looks familiar. Can you see it?" Mrs. Remington asked. "I'm sure there's a resemblance."

Mrs. Meyers bent over and stared at me. I looked down in embarrassment.

"My goodness gracious, is it really true?" Mrs. Meyers asked.

"It is," Mrs. Remington said. "Can't you tell by the voice, the look? She's even as tiny as her mother."

"My mother?" I gasped. "You knew my mother?"

"Was your mother Vicki Roberts?" Mrs. Meyers asked.

"No, her name was Victoria—wait, that's the same, isn't it?"

"Are you her daughter?" Mrs. Meyers asked.

"I think I am. I was told that Victoria Roberts was my mother. You knew her?" I asked.

"Of course I knew her," Mrs. Meyers said. "She worked here as a maid."

"We all knew her and *loved* her," Mrs. Remington said.

I gasped again. "But how is it possible that I'm here now?"

"That's my doing. Your matron, Mrs. Hazelton, contacted a dear friend of mine about the possibility of a young girl returning here, a girl of almost eighteen."

"But there are lots of girls my age."

"Not who were born here, not who were orphaned through tragedy, not who shared a birthdate with the little girl who left us," Mrs. Remington said. "I knew it had to be you."

"It has to be," Mrs. Meyers said. "When I look at you, I see her. You really do look like your mother."

I shook my head. "I wouldn't know. I've never even seen a picture of her."

Mrs. Meyers burst into laughter. "Tonight, after dinner, you'll see pictures of her and of you."

"Me?"

"After you were born, it was hard to take a photograph of one of you without the other," Mrs. Meyers said.

"I think I might have a few pictures in my albums too," Mrs. Remington said. "Do you think I could be part of it?"

"Of course you can!" Mrs. Meyers exclaimed. "If that's all right with Lizzy...I mean, Elizabeth."

"Of course it is, of course. The more the merrier."

"You know, that's something your mother might have said," Mrs. Meyers said.

"No," Mrs. Remington said. "That's something I know she *did* say. Let's finish dinner and move on to the more important part."

Seven

I SAT ON my bed the next morning, looking at the pictures they'd given me and going over in my head the stories they'd told me. It wasn't just Mrs. Meyers and Mrs. Remington—Nigel and James had joined us too. Each had stories that went along with the pictures. And now here I was, sitting in the room where my mother used to sleep, looking at pictures of her and of me. This was all so much, so quickly, that I was having trouble absorbing all of it.

Only two days ago I was living in an orphanage in Hope. My best friend—my sister—Toni and I shared a room. My name was Betty Shirley and I knew nothing about my mother—not her name or what she looked like or what had happened to her—or about my past. Now I was Elizabeth Anne—Lizzy Roberts— and I lived in Kingston, in a room that had been my mother's. I'd seen dozens of pictures of her and a little girl they said was me, and I knew far more about my history than I ever thought was possible.

When I saw the photographs, I knew why I had looked familiar to everyone. My mother could have been me, with a slightly different hairstyle and slightly lighter hair. That's what made it so difficult to comprehend. I could almost believe that the pictures were of me *and* a little girl rather than me *being* the little girl.

Of course I'd never had any pictures of the time before I came to the orphanage, and there were very few pictures of me taken since then. An occasional snapshot of a group of us or a class picture. Those were the only pictures I was in, and now they were all gone, destroyed in the fire.

There was one picture they'd given me that stood out. I'd stared at it before going to sleep—although sleep had been hard to come by—and dreamed about it. It was a picture that seemed more real than the others, as if I could remember it. It was taken only a few weeks before my mother's death, so I was almost four. I guess it made sense that if there was any picture I could remember, this would be it.

It was taken on the grounds of the property, with a little house in the background. I was told it was the guest cottage, the place where my mother and I had lived after my birth. The Remingtons, rather than asking her to leave when she had me, had made a place for us, and the staff had been like my family. They all had tales to tell about me—my first steps, first words, funny things I had done or said. It was all so wonderful and unreal and overwhelming.

In the picture, my mother was holding me by the hand. In the other hand, I held a doll. Something about that doll seemed instantly familiar. And then I remembered. Her name was Rosie. She was unmistakable. This was the doll I'd brought to the orphanage, the doll I'd always had with me with when I was little. I hadn't known where Rosie had come from, but I'd practically loved her to death. She was always being accidentally banged and bruised, and more than once Mrs. Hazelton had repaired a rip or even a torn limb.

As we both got older, Rosie had stopped going everywhere with me and I'd placed her on the top of my dresser. Over the past few years she had slept in my bottom dresser drawer. I hadn't held Rosie for years, but I'd always known she was there. That's where she'd been when we fled our room ahead of the fire. In hindsight I felt bad that I hadn't brought Rosie as we stumbled out of the Home. I had not rescued her.

I ran my finger against the picture, touching the doll the only way I could.

There was something about the picture. My mother was smiling—we were both smiling—but there was something else. I brought the picture up close and stared directly into her eyes. Her mouth was smiling, but her eyes weren't. There was a hint of worry. No, it was more than worry—it was fear. As if she knew what was going to happen.

I wished I could have been there to reassure her or warn her. But wait—I *was* there. That was me, that little girl standing beside her and holding her hand, smiling and carefree. Neither of us could have known what was going to happen only a few weeks later. And there was one thing I didn't understand. I was told we'd lived in the guest cottage, but when my mother was killed, we were living someplace else. That's what the newspaper article said—*the backyard of the house where the victim resided with her daughter, at the corner of Charles and Montreal*. Why were we living there instead of here? Why had we moved?

It was still early—just before seven in the morning. I had another hour before I had to report to the kitchen. There was plenty of time to get ready and to do something else as well.

I climbed out of bed and quickly changed into my clothes, slipping on my shoes. I opened the door to my room and then went back to get the picture. The house was silent, and I tried to move quietly, without disturbing or alerting anybody. I took a few steps in one direction before I realized I was going the wrong way. The house was so big and there were so many passages. Coming to the kitchen, I could hear the sounds of movement and activity. I passed by the entrance and caught sight of Nigel, his back to me, working at the counter. He didn't see me as I quickly walked past, heading for the back door. Stepping outside, I closed the door behind me and took a deep breath, filling my lungs with air. It was fresh and clean and cool.

The grounds were large, with well-tended flower beds, rich green lawns and manicured red-gravel paths. A large fountain stood in the center of the garden, and there were also a couple of smaller buildings and, in the back corner, what I thought was the guest cottage. I held up the picture to compare. It was unmistakable. This was the background of the last picture taken of my mother and me.

I walked until I was standing in front of the cottage. I looked at the picture again, trying to position myself as closely as possible to where it was taken. I looked back and forth from the picture to the cottage, shuffling a little in one direction and then another until it felt like I was in the exact spot. Maybe I thought standing there would bring me closer to my mother. I looked down; in my hand was the picture and not my doll. The other hand was empty. Standing where my mother had been standing was—nobody. If I was hoping for magic in that moment, I wasn't feeling it. I was just feeling alone.

"Good morning, Lizzy," a man said.

I looked up, startled and jumped slightly backward.

"Sorry," he said.

The man was older, maybe in his forties or even fifties, unshaven and dressed in work clothing, and he held a shovel. He had a smile on his face, but he was standing too close to me, and he was as big as I was small. He towered over me, making me feel uneasy. I'd met all the other staff already, so this had to be Ralph, the gardener.

"I didn't mean to scare you," he said.

"It's not your fault. I guess I'm just a little jumpy, and I wasn't paying attention."

"You were paying attention to whatever is in your hand. What is it?"

His voice was very mechanical. There was something strange about it—about him.

"It's a picture."

"Can I see it?" he asked, reaching out his free hand.

I hesitated for a split second, then handed it to him.

"I took this picture," he said.

"You did?"

"I like pictures. I like cameras. I have seven of them. If you'd like some pictures taken, I can take them."

"Thank you. I'm surprised you remember taking the picture."

"I remember all the pictures I've taken. It's like they're up here," he said, tapping a finger against the side of his head. "I liked taking pictures of your mother. She was very pretty." He scrunched up his face like he was thinking. "You look like her...you are very pretty."

"Thank you," I said. I was getting more uncomfortable. "The gardens are very pretty too."

"Yes, they are."

"You've done a great job. You're a very good gardener."

"I'm not the gardener. Ralph is the gardener."

"Oh, I thought you were Ralph." Now I felt even more uneasy. Who was this man? I looked around for somebody—anybody—else, but we were alone in the back of the garden, just the top of the main house visible. "Who are you?"

"I'm Richie."

"Richard Remington?" I asked.

He nodded his head. "I'm the oldest son. You can call me Richie—everybody does."

"Oh, I'm pleased to meet you, Richie. I'm sorry for thinking you were the gardener."

He shrugged. "Ralph is a good gardener. He's my friend. He's nice to my pigeons. Would you like to see my pigeons?"

I didn't want to say yes, but I didn't want to offend him. "I'd like to see them, but I don't think I have time now. I have to get back and help with breakfast."

He looked at his watch. "There is time for a short visit. Come."

Before I could object, he turned on his heels and started walking. I had no choice, did I? He was my employer's son. Then I remembered something James, the driver, had said about Richard: *He's friendly enough and completely harmless.* Trailing behind Richard, I hoped that was true.

He stopped and held open the door to a fancy little house. This couldn't be the coop, could it? I hesitated at the door and looked inside. I could see pigeons.

"Thank you," I said and stepped in.

There was a large cage filled with birds. A couple fluttered across the open area in the center of it, but most sat on little perches around the outer edge.

Richie closed the door behind him and then opened up the wire door that led into the cage. He stepped inside and motioned for me to join him. I hesitated.

"Don't worry," he said. "Birds never hurt anybody."

Reluctantly, I again did what he asked. He leaned his shovel against the mesh and then reached into his pocket and pulled out a handful of seed. Within seconds, birds were flying over and perching on his hand and arm, pushing each other out of the way to get at the seed.

"Aren't they pretty?" he asked.

"Very pretty, and there are so many different types." They were various sizes and colors, and some looked as if they were wearing feather hats or overcoats.

"Some are show pigeons—different types of rock pigeons that are bred to have different characteristics. I also have homing pigeons. Would you like to know all of their names?"

Before I could answer, he started to rattle them off. If he hadn't been so serious, and so many of the pigeons distinctive, I would have thought he was making them up as he went.

"You don't have to know all their names," he said.

"That's good," I said. I didn't think I could correctly name a single one.

He continued talking about them. As he did, he'd stroke the back of one or make sure another got more seed. He was so caring toward his birds, so gentle, that I knew he had to be gentle and caring toward people too.

"Do you think I could feed them?" I asked.

He broke into a gigantic smile and reached into his pocket and pulled out some seed. He placed it in my outstretched hand. Almost instantly a pigeon lit on my arm. I worked to stay steady and still. It pecked at the seed and that seemed to signal to the other pigeons that it was safe, and another four fluttered over and settled onto my arm.

"They like you," he said.

"They like seed."

"They like both. Pigeons know people. They won't take feed from somebody who's bad. They know you're nice."

"Then they must think you're even nicer," I said.

He looked away, and I could see that he was blushing. I hadn't meant to embarrass him.

"You know a lot about pigeons," I said, changing the topic.

"No, not a lot. I know *everything* about pigeons. Everything. Go ahead, ask me a question, any question."

I didn't really know enough to even ask a question. "Um…how many pigeons do you have?"

"I have thirty-five fancy pigeons and twelve homing pigeons."

"Thanks for letting me see them. I better get inside now and help with breakfast."

"You can come back if you'd like," he said.

"That would be nice. I will come back."

"Your mother liked to come out here. She even went to some races with me."

"Races?"

"Some of us drive our birds far away, more than a hundred miles, and then we see which birds return fastest," he explained.

"That's interesting. Do they always come back?"

"Almost always, but sometimes one or two get caught by a falcon."

"That's awful."

"It's sad, but even falcons have to live. People have been racing pigeons for thousands of years. They are very good athletes, and I have the best birds in the county, probably the whole province."

He started talking to the birds, making cooing sounds and giving one a little kiss. It was almost as if I suddenly wasn't there. I'd just slip out and—

"Would you like to come and see them racing sometime?" he asked.

"I don't get much time off. Just Sundays and Monday afternoon."

"We only race them on Sunday. So you'll come with me?"

I nodded. "I'll come with you."

"That will be nice. The pigeons will be happy. I will be happy."

Eight

I BROUGHT DOWN the last of the lunch dishes. Lunch had been set for four, as was each and every meal, although Mrs. Remington was usually the only person who dined. She was friendly and asked questions of both Mrs. Meyers and me. Classical music played in the background. It reminded me of my times with Mrs. Hazelton, which made me happy and sad at the same time.

I set the tray down on the counter beside the sink where Nigel was washing dishes.

"Do you want me to put away the dishes that weren't used?" I asked.

"Just leave them here and join the others for lunch."

"Yes, join us!" James called out.

He and Mrs. Meyers and Ralph, the gardener, who was a little man half the size of Richie, were sitting at the table in the corner. We'd be having the same lunch as Mrs. Remington. Since food had been prepared for four and eaten only by one, there was more than enough for all of us to eat.

I sat down beside Mrs. Meyers, and she prepared a plate for me.

"So I hear you met our Richie today," James said.

"He showed me his pigeons."

"Was he carrying his shovel?" James asked.

"Yes, he was."

"No surprise there. He always has his shovel with him these days."

"Lord knows why he's become so attached to that shovel," Mrs. Meyers said.

"He does use it to clean the pigeon coop," Ralph said. "But still."

"Do you remember when he'd only wear that one sweater?" James said.

"Or only eat from one particular plate, although I couldn't tell one from another," Nigel added.

"It's always one thing or another with him," Mrs. Meyers said. "From when he was a boy. If it wasn't a blanket, it was a toy or a train. Harmless enough."

"Unless you tried to take it away from him," Ralph said. "That can cause more than a little bit of a fuss."

"He told me he had the best racing pigeons in the entire county," I said.

"He should have," Ralph said. "Whenever somebody beats him, he buys the bird from them."

"No matter the price," James said. "People have learned that, and they jack the price up."

"That's terrible."

"Thank goodness his brother's been able to intervene and convince people to accept a fair price and not take advantage of Richie," Mrs. Meyers said. "Edward really is his brother's keeper."

"That's one way to describe him," James said.

"Richie invited me to go to one of the races," I added.

"It isn't much to see. A bunch of birds are released and the time of release is recorded," James said.

"How does that make it a race?"

"The time of their arrival to their home coops is recorded, their speed is calculated, and the winners are declared the next day," James said. "Funny how some of the *winners* never fly as fast once they become part of Richie's stable."

"I'm sure some people are cheating him by recording false times," Mrs. Meyers said. "And more would do the same if it wasn't for his brother."

"I think most people know better than to play fast and loose with the mayor. I wouldn't want to get on his wrong side," James said.

"He's only doing what's right," Mrs. Meyers said.

James didn't say anything, but judging from his expression, there was more he wanted to say. "The next race is in three weeks, so I guess you'll be joining us," James said.

"You drive?" I asked, feeling instantly better.

"Richie doesn't drive anymore," James said.

"And that's a good thing," Ralph added. "What with the accidents and all."

"He wasn't the best driver," Mrs. Meyers said.

"When I drive, he's always checking to make sure I don't speed. He insists I go exactly the speed limit and stop exactly three seconds at stop signs. He counts them out."

"Sounds like he doesn't trust your driving," Ralph said with a laugh.

"Thirty-two years without an accident or a speeding ticket," James said.

"Come on, what policeman is going to give the mayor's mother's driver a speeding ticket?" Nigel asked.

He finished the dishes and sat down to join us.

"He wasn't always the mayor," James said.

"But he always was rich—or, at least, the family was. Would you have wanted to be the policeman to cross old man Remington?" Nigel asked.

"Point taken," James agreed.

"As it is now, Richie hardly ever leaves the grounds except for those races."

I wanted to ask one more question, but I was afraid of offending someone.

James saved me the trouble. "You're probably wondering what's wrong with him, aren't you?"

"Yes."

"I wish I could give you an answer," he said. "He's just odd."

"Very odd," Ralph said.

"It's not that he isn't smart," Mrs. Meyers said. "He was reading before he was in school, and he knows everything there is to know about some things."

"Things like pigeons and watches," James said.

"And trains. Don't forget trains. Big ones and model ones," Ralph said.

"He does know his trains," Mrs. Meyers said. "It's just that he's not so good with people."

James snorted. "Not so good?" He laughed. "It's as if relationships are foreign languages to him."

"He's always had trouble with people," Mrs. Meyers said. "He was always an odd little duckie, but we hoped he'd outgrow it."

"At least he's finally outgrown the fighting," James said.

"There's no need to bring that up," Mrs. Meyers said. "It's been more than a decade." She turned to me. "It was more a misunderstanding than anything else, and it was so long ago. We don't want to make Lizzy afraid of him."

"I'm not afraid. He seems kind and gentle."

"He is gentle," Mrs. Meyers said.

"And that's a good thing, because he's as strong as an ox," James said.

"That he is," Ralph confirmed. "I've seen him pick up a bag of bird feed that weighs over a hundred pounds and toss it like it's nothing."

"I've also seen him pick up a little girl and toss her a dozen feet into the air and then catch her. Do you remember that?" Mrs. Meyers asked me.

I shook my head.

"You better not remind Richie of that—he could still toss you up pretty high," James joked.

"No need to remind him—you know he remembers everything," Mrs. Meyers said. "He has the memory of an elephant."

"It's almost frightening," Nigel said. "He can tell you what he ate for breakfast three months ago."

I thought of his telling me about the picture, and how he remembered every picture he'd ever taken.

"That's part of how his mind works. He seems to store information like that. Things the rest of us forget, he remembers," Mrs. Meyers said. "He could probably tell you things about you and your mother that the rest of us have forgotten. He used to spend a lot of time with you."

"I didn't know that." There was so much I didn't know.

"The two of you used to play all the time," Mrs. Meyers said. "Now that I think of it, I remember the two of you sitting at a little table, having afternoon tea with your dolls."

I remembered that! It was like a dream that now was real. I could picture sun shining through the window, the table set with little pink plastic plates and cups, my dolls sitting at the chairs, and there was a man...was it Richie?

"So now you only have one more member of the Remington family to meet," James said. "His Worship himself is going to be gracing us at dinner tonight."

"He is?" Mrs. Meyers asked.

"I've been asked to pick him up from city hall in time for dinner, although that doesn't mean he's actually going to come," James said.

"He's a very busy man," Mrs. Meyers said. "Being the mayor of a city as large as Kingston is a very demanding job. I know how happy it always makes Mrs. Remington to have him for dinner. Let's put on our *very* best tonight."

Nine

THE SOUP HAD already been served, and Mrs. Remington was still the only person seated for dinner. The other three places were set but unused. She was trying to put on a brave face, but it wasn't hard to see that she was disappointed, even a little sad. It must have been lonely, always eating by herself. It was so much better to be part of a family—the way I had been back at the orphanage. We hadn't had fancy plates and silverware or candles on the table, or even fancy food on our plates, but we'd had each other. There was always talking and giggling, and even the occasional harsh word was better than silence. I wondered if Mrs. Remington had music on in the background so that she would feel less alone.

For the first time since arriving, I felt sorry for her. She was rich and had everything money could buy, but really she didn't have much at all. One son was out in the yard with his pigeons and shovel, and the second wasn't going to come—exactly as James had predicted. I guessed we'd all be eating well that evening, dining on the leftovers.

"Good evening, Mother. I'm so sorry for being tardy!"

Edward—it had to be Edward—swept into the room. He didn't so much enter as make an entrance.

"It's so wonderful to see you, my son!" Mrs. Remington called out. She beamed as he bent over and gave her a big hug.

"I just wish I could have gotten away sooner, but there were pressing matters."

"The important thing is that you're here now," Mrs. Remington said.

He was tall and slender, dressed in a black suit, a red tie and shiny shoes. He was distinguished-looking, as you'd expect the mayor to be. But more than that, he was *so* handsome. If somebody had told me he was a movie star, I would have believed them. He sat down at the seat beside his mother, reached out and took her hand in his.

"So tell me, what has my dear mother been up to these past few days?" he asked. "Fill me in—tell me everything."

"Oh, that's not worth talking about. My days are all pretty much the same. How about you, my son?"

"Busy as always, between fulfilling the duties of the mayor's office and tending to family business. Which reminds me, I have a few papers for you to sign." He pulled them out of the pocket of his jacket. "But let's not talk business now. Surely there must be something new that's happened?"

"Well, yes, it's not some*thing* new, but some*body* new," she said. "Or, really, not new so much as newly returned."

I realized she was talking about me, and suddenly I felt very self-conscious.

"Lizzy, I'd like to reintroduce you to my son, Edward."

He looked up and greeted me with a warm, open smile that made my nervous feelings vanish. I walked over to Mrs. Remington's side.

"Oh, my goodness," he said. "It is unmistakable. You look so much like your mother."

"So I'm told." And now that I had seen the pictures, I knew it was true.

"It's as if somebody has turned back the hands of time. Same eyes, same smile, even the same voice."

"She *does* sound like her mother," Mrs. Remington said. "Exactly."

"And she is exactly as beautiful."

Mrs. Remington chuckled. "I think both my boys had a little crush on her."

"I think it's safe to say that she was loved by everybody, including you and both of your boys." He turned to me. "Your mother was a flower, one whose life was ended far too soon."

I felt like I'd been kicked in the stomach. My legs suddenly felt wobbly, and it must have showed. Edward jumped to his feet, took me by the arm and eased me into a chair.

"Get her something to drink!" he ordered.

Mrs. Meyers came forward and placed a glass of water in my hand.

"What happened? What happened?" Mrs. Remington cried out.

"Your son was an insensitive twit is what happened," Edward said. He got down on one knee and looked directly into my eyes. "Please forgive me."

"I'm fine…honestly."

"You were going to faint. Take a drink of water," he said.

I took a little sip and then a bigger one. I felt better. I went to get up, and he placed a hand on my shoulder.

"Take a minute. Please, don't make me feel any worse than I do now."

"There's nothing for you to feel badly for. I'm just overly tired. I haven't slept much since all of this happened." That was true.

"Mrs. Meyers, bring her a little something to nibble on," Mrs. Remington said. "You've had a touch of the vapors," she said to me.

As quickly as the water had appeared, a bowl of soup was placed in front of me.

"Now, dear mother, I assume it was no fortuitous turn of fate that brought Lizzy back into our midst but was more your hand. Is that correct?"

"I still have a few connections," Mrs. Remington said.

"A few? I won't even bother asking what machinations you undertook. I'm just grateful. I wish to make a toast.

Mrs. Meyers, come and join us." He poured wine into a glass and then topped up his mother's glass and his own.

"Raise your drinks. To my dear mother for bending fate, and to the return of our Lizzy. Welcome home."

Ten

I RUBBED THE polish off the spoon, held it up and examined it. It shone so brightly that I could catch a distorted vision of myself in it.

In the background was the faint sound of classical music. I didn't recognize the piece, but I had a feeling it was Bach. There was a certain intricacy, a layered, almost mechanical quality. Not that I meant *mechanical* in a bad way; it was a precision I found comforting. Anything I knew about music was taught to me by Mrs. Hazelton as we sat in her office.

I picked up another spoon. I didn't know how many I'd done or how many were left to do, but Mrs. Meyers had told me there was enough silverware to have a formal dinner party for sixty people. That was a lot of knives and spoons and forks, and then there were dozens and dozens of serving spoons, tongs, spatulas and flippers. On top of that, there were silver napkin rings, salt and pepper shakers, serving bowls and a dozen candelabras, each of which held six candles. I couldn't even imagine how much all of this had cost, but I knew it was an amount far beyond what I'd ever earn.

Even if I had the money, I wouldn't spend it on a bunch of silverware. How many forks and knives did you need? What was the point in having all of this when it wasn't ever used? Wouldn't it be better to have sixty friends rather than cutlery for sixty people who never showed up?

"You seem to be enjoying the music."

I startled slightly and turned to face Mrs. Remington standing in the doorway. I had been so absorbed I hadn't heard her enter.

"You were humming along," she added.

"Sorry if I disturbed you."

"You didn't disturb me. Human voices are always a welcome sound in this house."

"I like Bach," I said.

"Do you have a favorite?"

"Cello Suite No. 1 and maybe the Toccata and Fugue in D Minor."

"Classics. This piece, on the other hand, is very obscure. Do you know it?"

"No, ma'am."

"But you knew it was Bach."

"I can tell Bach. He's just so *precise*."

"He is that, although I think I prefer the romantic era," she said.

"Like Beethoven?"

"Yes, exactly. He bridged the gap between the more purely classical and the romantic eras and—you do know your music."

"Mrs. Hazelton thought it was an important part of our education."

"I believe I would like your Mrs. Hazelton. Have you written to her to tell her how you've settled in?"

I shook my head, feeling embarrassed. I'd meant to do it, but I hadn't gotten around to it. I needed to send a letter to Toni too. I was busy, but I knew it was more than that. I didn't know exactly what to say. So much had happened, and I wasn't sure how to put it down in writing.

"You've been here for two weeks, so you should have an idea if you are enjoying your position," Mrs. Remington said.

"I am enjoying it! Everybody has been so nice. Mrs. Meyers, James, Nigel, Ralph and you."

"And my son?"

"Richie has been more than nice. He's told me so many stories about my mother and me. He remembers *everything*."

"He does have a remarkable memory. Our family physician—who passed away many years ago—used the term photographic, or eidetic, memory. It refers to the ability to recall things accurately and vividly, and Richie certainly has that. Sometimes, though, having a memory like that is more curse than blessing."

"I don't understand."

"There are certain things that it's best not to remember. Having you here has brought back many wonderful memories, but I have to admit that others are, well, just so terrible."

Of course I knew what she meant.

"The death of your mother was such a horrendous thing for all of us. Edward was terribly upset; he didn't come out of his room for a week. I think in some way he almost felt responsible for what happened."

"Why would he feel responsible?"

"It's just his way. He's always been such a responsible person. He takes the weight of the world on his shoulders. Thank goodness he's as strong as his father was. He thought if he could have convinced your mother not to quit her job and move the two of you away, it wouldn't have happened."

"Why did we move away?"

"Your mother said it was time for the two of you to leave, to get on with your lives. How sad that it didn't involve getting on with her life but ending it."

Again I felt as if I'd been struck.

"Perhaps that's why I'm feeling guilty. If only I'd been able to persuade her to stay." She covered her face with her hands, and I thought she had started to cry. I knew I was close to it myself.

I walked over and put my hand on her shoulder. "I know you tried your best."

She looked up and put her hand on top of mine. "I didn't try hard enough. I should have *made* her stay. Not just for her and for you, but for Richie. I've never seen him more distraught than he was over the whole thing. It's not that he doesn't have emotions, but he usually keeps them inside. The day your mother left, he let those emotions out." She shook her head. "I can't talk about this anymore. It's still very raw, even after all this time."

She let out a big sigh, and I could tell she was trying to force herself not to cry.

"I'm going to go to the pigeon races with Richie next weekend," I said.

"You are very kind to him. Do you know if Richie had lunch?"

"I'm not sure. I've been polishing the silver all morning."

"The silver can wait. Go and talk to Mrs. Meyers, and if he hasn't eaten, take him his lunch."

"Yes, ma'am."

I started to leave and she called me back. "Lizzy, you really are so much like your mother."

I'd heard that often over the past two weeks, but it was reassuring and it seemed to bring me closer to my mother.

ce

I carried the tray across the lawn. Richie hadn't eaten, and Mrs. Meyers had been getting his lunch ready when I entered the kitchen and told her I'd been asked to take it to him.

I poked my head into the coop. The birds were cooing; they sounded very content. And then I heard Richie talking. I took a few steps inside and saw him in the corner. He was sitting on a stool, a couple of birds on his shoulders, his silver shovel leaning against the wall.

While I could hear him, I couldn't make out what he was saying. There was a soothing quality to his voice, quiet and calm. Strangely, whenever he talked to or about his birds, his voice seemed more natural, less mechanical. I cleared my throat, and he turned around.

"Hello, Lizzy."

His voice was back to sounding mechanical.

"I brought you lunch." I put it down on the table and almost instantly two pigeons fluttered over and perched on the edge of the tray. They knew there was food under the covers.

His clothing, as always, was stained with pigeon droppings. I knew that because doing laundry was my responsibility. I'd started to think that he should only wear white shirts, so that it didn't show so much.

He stood over his food, lowered his head and closed his eyes. He always said a prayer before eating. I put my head down too. A few extra prayers wouldn't hurt.

I asked for protection for Toni and all of the other girls. I asked for healing for Mrs. Hazelton. I asked for guidance as more of my past was revealed to me. I asked for speed for Richie's pigeons in the coming race, and then I heard him say, "Amen" and I did the same.

"Were you praying for your mother?" he asked.

His question shocked me. I didn't know what to say or how to react.

"Today is the day," he said.

What did he mean? Oh my goodness…he didn't mean the day that—

"This is your mother's birthday."

"My mother's birthday!"

He nodded his head. "Today. She was born in 1925."

"I didn't know that." I hadn't thought to even wonder when she was born. Over the past weeks I had been flooded with information, and I was swimming in a sea of other people's stories and recollections. Really, though, it wasn't much. There was so much I still didn't know. So much more that everybody had to offer—maybe Richie more so than anyone.

"Are you going to visit?" Richie asked.

"Visit who?"

"Your mother."

My heart skipped a beat.

"Are you going to the cemetery?"

I shook my head. "I wasn't planning to."

"You should. We always go on my father's birthday."

"I don't even know where she's buried."

"I do. I could take you."

I wanted to go, but I didn't want to go right now. Not this second.

"Maybe we could go on Sunday after the pigeon race," I suggested.

He shook his head. "It isn't your mother's birthday on Sunday. It's her birthday today."

"But James isn't here. He told me he had to take the car in for service." I was looking for an excuse.

"It isn't far. We can walk."

"But I'm working. I have the rest of the silverware to polish."

"My mother would let you go."

The last of my excuses had been stripped away. What else could I say? "Do you want to go later today?"

"I'll eat, and then we should go. I'll tell my mother we're going."

Eleven

I STOOD AT the front door, waiting for Richie. No one had objected to my taking the time off. In fact, Mrs. Remington had not only agreed but had asked Ralph to pick two big, beautiful bunches of flowers. One for my mother and one for Mrs. Remington's husband, Richie's father. I hadn't realized they were buried in the same place, but really, how many cemeteries could there be in Kingston, especially close to here?

"Are you going to be all right, dearie?" Mrs. Meyers asked.

"I'm fine."

"Richie will take care of you." She paused. "You also need to take care of him."

I wasn't sure how I was supposed to do that.

She added, "He'll be fine, I'm sure. It's just that sometimes strangers can be a bit off-putting. I know you'll take care of it."

I wasn't so sure, but I appreciated the vote of confidence.

"And here's Richie now," Mrs. Meyers said.

He still had on the same stained shirt and tattered pants and was carrying his shovel, but he was wearing a tie now. It was much too short and hung awkwardly around his neck.

Mrs. Meyers straightened his tie. "You take care of Lizzy, okay?"

"Yes, ma'am."

He was always so respectful to Mrs. Meyers. He started walking away, and I hurried to catch up to him.

*   ℮

We came to the fence marking the edge of the cemetery. I could make out the headstones, stretching into the distance as far as I could see. It was a large cemetery. It had taken us less than fifteen minutes to walk here, and I was grateful, since we'd certainly been attracting a lot of attention. Cars slowed down so people could gawk at us—a large man carrying a shiny silver shovel, and a girl with two gigantic bouquets of flowers.

Of course, it would have been much worse if they hadn't been friendly. Dozens of people in passing cars honked their horns and waved or yelled, "Hey, Richie" from open windows. People on their front porches called out greetings, as did the few people we passed on the sidewalk. It shouldn't have surprised me that everybody knew Richie. He'd lived here his whole life, and he certainly was distinctive, maybe more so because his family was so prominent.

Richie hardly seemed to notice the attention. A couple of times he awkwardly waved a hand in response, but mostly it was as if he didn't notice. I tried to fill in for him, smiling or nodding and waving a bouquet of flowers in reply. I was feeling uncomfortable enough for both of us.

I also got the idea that he hardly noticed me. I tried to start a conversation, but he didn't seem to want to talk at all. I even asked him about his pigeons—which was usually good for a long conversation—but he didn't bite. And as much as he didn't seem to want to talk, I wanted to. I wanted something to ease the uncomfortable feeling in my stomach, which seemed to be getting worse as we walked. I was past nervous. I felt scared. Not scared like I was a kid going to a spooky cemetery. It was something more. I felt like I should have had more time to prepare—but prepare for what?

I kept looking to the side, through the fence. There were so many headstones, so many people who had passed on. Richie stopped, as did I. We stood at the gates. The plaque on the post said *Cataraqui Cemetery*. I wondered why we had stopped. Richie had his head down, his eyes closed, his lips moving slightly. He was praying again.

Richie said, "Amen," and we walked through the open gates. Suddenly, my feeling of unease became a gigantic knot in my stomach. I didn't want to follow him any farther.

Richie kept on walking, not noticing I wasn't with him. Finally I ran after him, not stopping until I was right beside him. He looked over and gave me a little smile. It wasn't much, but it was reassuring. I wasn't doing this alone.

I just wished I was with Mrs. Hazelton or Toni or Joe or, I guess, any of the girls. Of course, that wasn't possible.

"The prime minister," Richie said.

I looked around. I didn't see anybody, and I couldn't imagine why the prime minister would be here. Then I saw that Richie was pointing at a tall headstone behind a small black fence.

"A prime minister is buried here?" I asked.

He nodded.

"Which one?"

"Sir John Alexander Macdonald. Born in Glasgow, Scotland, January 11, 1815. Moved to Kingston at age five with his family. First prime minister, serving from 1867 to 1871. Second term from 1872 through 1873. Third and fourth terms from 1878 to 1887. Formed his fifth and sixth governments from 1887 until his death on June 6, 1891, at age seventy-six."

I knew that everything he said must be correct because he was always right with his facts.

"His headstone is the second biggest in the entire cemetery," Richie said.

"Who has one that's bigger?"

"My father. In his will he asked that it be one inch higher and one inch wider than the prime minister's monument," Richie said.

I chuckled and then suppressed my laughter. "And nobody has built a bigger one since then?" I asked.

"Nobody is allowed to. My mother made sure that will never happen. It's like a law because she's on the cemetery board."

That was strange, that old Mr. Remington wanted his headstone to be the biggest, even bigger than the first prime minister's. Even stranger that it would always be the biggest. I shouldn't have been surprised though. Mrs. Remington was kind, and she was also dedicated to the memory of her husband, and I knew there was real substance and power beneath that kindness.

"Should we go to your father's first or my..." I let the sentence trail off. I couldn't bring myself to say the word *mother*. It felt foreign to me.

"Your mother," he said. "To visit Vicki."

He led and I followed. The cemetery was well maintained. The grass was green and mowed. Many of the graves had tended flower beds or, at least, flowers that had been placed there. There had been nobody to put flowers on my mother's grave all these years. That made me sad. I pulled the flowers close to my chest. I was glad I had brought them.

There were so many stones, so many graves. Some were large and magnificent. Others were just small stones lying flat on the ground. That's what my mother's would look like, I was sure. Some of the stones were so old that they were worn and weathered, and I couldn't make out what was written on them. On others the writing was clear, and I could see dates of birth and death, inscriptions, a few words to sum up a life and a death. *Loved, Missed, Mother, Father, Gone on to Heaven*, along with a Bible passage and maybe a little saying. What would be written on my mother's stone? Would the letters even stand out?

Richie stopped in front of a large pink headstone. I wondered why he was stopping here, and then I saw. It was my mother's grave.

Victoria Audrey Roberts
Born July 12, 1925
Tragically Taken September 10, 1950
Daughter of Samuel and Doris Roberts
Mother of Elizabeth Anne

I felt my legs go weak. I hadn't even thought about the inscription or known what I'd expected to see, but I hadn't expected to see my name. There was one more line below my name, and I read it out loud.

"*An angel returned to Heaven*," I said. "That's so…so beautiful."

"My brother wrote that," Richie said.

"That was sweet of him." I would have to thank him the next time he came for dinner. "I hadn't expected the stone to be so big."

"It's not as big as my father's."

"Nobody's is. I just meant, well, who paid for it?"

"My mother. She said Vicki deserved to have the best."

I should have known. That act of kindness was so much like Mrs. Remington. I had to thank her as well.

The stone wasn't just big but also beautiful. There were flowers carved in a delicate pattern and, in each corner, a small angel. It must have cost a lot of money.

"I wish I could have been here," I said.

"You were."

"I didn't know."

"I held you. We stood over there," he said. He pointed off to the side.

I tried to remember but couldn't. I wanted to remember. "Can you tell me more?"

"I can tell you almost everything. My mother and brother and James and Nigel and Ralph and Mrs. Meyers and some other people you don't know were here. Reverend Simpson gave the eulogy. He was a nice man. He died the next year on August 23."

"Is there anything more you can tell me?"

"It was cold and the wind was strong, so I took you where it was sheltered and I put you under my coat so that just your head was showing and—"

"I remember! Well...I think I remember some of it."

"You put down a flower—a rose, the flower your mother liked best."

I tried to picture it, and then I saw that there was a rose—the remains of a single rose—at the base of the stone. That couldn't be it, could it? I looked closer. There were the faint remains of another flower, and then another and another. Little bits of flowers that had been placed here but couldn't possibly have survived for almost fourteen years.

I kneeled down and gently placed a bouquet on the ground, leaning against the stone. I reached out and touched it. Cold and smooth. Here, beneath that stone, under my feet, was my mother. I felt a shiver run through my body.

I ran my hand over to the place where my name was written. With one finger I traced the name—my name. Elizabeth Anne.

"You did that," Richie said. "You touched your name with your finger, just like that. You were learning to print your name, and you read it there."

I burst into tears. Richie bent down and patted me on the back. "There, there…there, there." The tears kept coming, and my whole body began to shake. I tried to stop myself, but I couldn't. Richie kept patting me on the back and saying, "There, there." He looked distressed, helpless, like he wanted to help me but didn't know what else he could do.

Really, at that moment there was nothing anybody could have done.

Twelve

WE WALKED SLOWLY toward the gates. I didn't know exactly what time it was, but we were in the cemetery a very long time before I managed to regain my composure. Or maybe I just didn't have any tears left to cry. I was drained. Richie had left me alone—at my insistence—to go visit his father's grave. I'd stayed beside my mother's, sitting on the grass, trying to remember and glad that I couldn't. What good would trying to remember do anyway? All it could do was bring more tears.

"Thank you for bringing me," I said as we left.

"You're welcome. Did you wish your mother a happy birthday?" he asked.

"Um…no."

"Do you want to go back?"

"No, I'm good. I'll go back another day."

Off to our side there was a funeral going on. A long line of cars was parked on the roadway, and a group of black-clad mourners huddled together. In some ways it was reassuring to have other people here, even if it meant that somebody had died. I couldn't help wondering who it was. I hoped it was somebody old, very old, and not some child or a mother who had a young child.

I was close enough to hear a voice but too far away to hear the words. I'd never been to a funeral before—well, one that I remembered. This was as close as I had ever come, and I wanted to get farther away.

We exited through the gates and started back the way we'd come. Suddenly there was a short siren blast. I turned around. A police car pulled up to the curb beside us and came to a stop.

"Excuse me!" a man called, leaning out the window.

I stopped and turned toward him, but Richie kept walking, as if he hadn't heard anything. The car moved forward until it came alongside Richie.

"Hey, you! Stop!" the officer ordered.

This time Richie looked right at him. There was no question that he had heard, but he didn't stop. He just kept walking—same speed and same stride. I quickened my pace to get to where the police car was, but once again it moved forward. This time, rather than simply coming alongside, the car bounced up onto the sidewalk ahead of Richie.

The officer jumped out. He was big but young. He couldn't have been that much older than me. He held up his hand.

"I ordered you to stop!" he called to Richie. His voice was loud, but there was a quiver in it.

Richie continued to move toward him. I rushed to his side and took him by the arm. "Wait," I said, stopping him just before he reached the policeman, who looked relieved that we'd stopped.

"I need to ask you a few questions," he said.

"Certainly," I said. I tried to smile, but instead a few more tears came out.

"Are you all right?" he asked me.

I nodded, but as I tried to answer, my voice broke on the first word. Now he looked worried instead of relieved.

"I need to know your name," he said to Richie, pointing a finger in his face.

Richie didn't answer.

"And I want you to put down that shovel right now."

I knew Richie wasn't about to give up his shovel.

"Put it down now!" the officer ordered again, his voice much louder. "Put it down! " This time it was a command.

"It's my shovel," Richie said. At least he'd spoken.

"I don't care who owns it. Put the weapon down!" The officer put one hand on the holster of his gun. What was he doing?

"It is his shovel; it really is! My name is Betty...I mean, Lizzy...I mean, Elizabeth Anne!"

"Which is it?" he asked.

"Both—all of them. It's hard to explain."

"Knowing your own name is seldom difficult unless it's a false name."

"It's not false, it's just that, well, it's really complicated."

"Has he hurt you?"

"No. Of course not! We just came out of the cemetery and—"

"I saw you come out of the cemetery. That's why I asked you to stop. Walking out of a cemetery with a shovel seems a little suspicious. I have a few questions and—"

Richie started walking again, moving around the officer and the car. The officer reached out to grab him, and Richie slapped away his hand and then, quick as a cat, swung the shovel. It went wide of the officer and smashed the police car's headlamp. I screamed, and the officer staggered backward and pulled out his gun. I jumped forward, putting myself between Richie and the officer.

"He didn't mean anything!" I yelled. "He doesn't know any better! He's different!"

The officer still held the gun at his side. He looked upset and, strangely, as scared as I was. He let out a big sigh, and slowly he seemed to relax. Then he slipped the revolver back into its holster.

"He can't just ignore a police officer. He can't just destroy police property, even if he is different," he said.

"If you come back to the house, I know Mrs. Remington will pay for it."

"Remington? Like the mayor?"

"That's her son. Her *other* son."

"That's the mayor's brother?" he asked as he pointed at Richie, who was walking away.

"His big brother. You can ask his mother. Just come back to the house, and she'll explain everything."

"I have a better idea," he said. "I better radio this in."

He jumped back into his car, and I rushed after Richie, who was already half a block away. As I reached Richie, the police car came up beside us again. The officer leaned out the window. "I'm sorry, really sorry, Mr. Remington...*really* sorry."

Richie turned and nodded at him and gave a little wave. Before I could think of anything to say, the car sped off.

"You shouldn't have done that," I said.

"Done what?"

"Hit the car."

"It shouldn't have been on the sidewalk. Cars shouldn't be on the sidewalk."

"He just wanted to talk to you."

"I didn't know him. I don't talk to people I don't know. He's gone now."

He was gone. But I didn't think we'd heard the last of it.

Thirteen

I WAS CLEARING away dishes from the first course of dinner when the doorbell rang. Mrs. Remington rarely had visitors, and they never came unannounced. Mainly it was Edward who visited. He'd come by on three occasions now. I'd been rehearsing in my head all afternoon what I'd say to him the next time I saw him. I wanted to thank him for what he had done for my mother—those words on her headstone. He was always so kind to me, but still I felt a little nervous around him. He was the mayor and—

The doorbell rang again.

"I wonder who that could be," Mrs. Remington said.

"Lizzy, could you please get the door?" Mrs. Meyers asked.

"Yes, ma'am."

I left the dining room and the Beethoven behind and hurried to the door as the bell rang for the third time.

Whoever it was, they were both persistent and impatient. "Coming, coming," I said to myself.

I threw open the door and it was that police officer, hat in hand. This couldn't be good.

"Hello, Betty, Lizzy, Elizabeth Anne," he said. His smile looked forced. "I'm here to speak to Mr. Remington and his mother."

"He didn't mean it. He really didn't, and I'm still sure that Mrs. Remington will pay for the damage!"

"The damage is being paid for. I'm here to offer an apology to Mr. Remington and his mother. Are they here?"

"They're here." Richie was in the backyard with his pigeons, and I didn't know if he'd come in. I might have to bring the officer out there.

"May I come in, please?"

"Yes, of course!" I opened the door wider, and he stepped inside. "Come this way."

I started toward the dining room. I didn't look back, but I could hear his big booted feet behind me. I pulled aside the curtain that led into the dining room and ushered him inside.

"Mrs. Remington, there's somebody here to see you," I said.

She looked up from her meal and to where I stood. "I can't see the face, but judging from the blue blur, I do believe that would be Officer Gibson."

"Yes, ma'am, it is."

How did she know his name?

"I received a phone call from both my son and your chief," she said. "I've known Ernie, your chief, since he was a baby. His family and my family are dear old friends."

"He told me that, ma'am, when he explained that I should come over here and ask you and your son to accept my apology."

"Well, that's absurd," Mrs. Remington said. "I will *not* accept your apology." She paused, and I felt the tension rise in the room, almost as if somebody had suddenly turned up the heat. "And the reason for that is because you do not owe me or my son an apology."

"I don't?"

"Of course not. You were just doing your job. You didn't know who Richie was."

"I've only been on the force for three months. I moved here for the job."

"Then how could you know? I hope Ernie wasn't too hard on you," she said.

"He was very, um, *certain* in his direction," Officer Gibson said.

"You put that very diplomatically. The stories I could tell you about your chief as a boy! I always thought he was more likely to end up on the other side of the equation— criminal instead of police chief. Who would have thought that those two, best friends as boys, would end up chief of police and mayor?"

"Certainly not me," Mrs. Meyers said quietly.

"I think Ernie and my son are simply naturally protective of Richie," Mrs. Remington said.

"Families and friends should be like that," Officer Gibson said. "I would do the same if it was my brother. I might have yelled at the police officer even louder."

"The boy became the man," Mrs. Meyers said, "and that boy—your chief—always seemed to be yelling."

"Regardless, ma'am, I am truly sorry for any trouble I caused you or your son. Perhaps I could extend my apology to him."

"I think the apology would trouble him even more. Lizzy explained what happened, and I know it wasn't that bad. It wasn't like you pulled a gun on him."

He looked at me, his eyes widening ever so slightly.

"No, ma'am," I said. I didn't know why I was lying for the officer, but maybe I thought I was protecting myself as well. I was supposed to look after Richie, and he'd had a firearm pulled on him. I felt as if it was as much my fault as Officer Gibson's.

"I was told there was some damage to the police car," Mrs. Remington said.

"Yes, ma'am, there was a smashed headlamp."

"Then I'll have somebody get my purse so we can pay for the repairs."

"It's all right, ma'am. It's been taken care of," he said.

"Taken care of? How?"

He paused before he said, "It will be coming out of my pay."

"Did you smash the headlamp?" she asked.

"No, ma'am."

"Then you will *not* be paying for it. Mrs. Meyers, could you please go and get my purse so that I can—"

"The chief was very insistent on that point," Officer Gibson said. "Very insistent."

"He can be as insistent as he wishes, but he is simply not going to tell me what I can and cannot do. He may be the chief of police, but I'm the mother of the mayor, and even the mayor—his boss—is wise enough to do as I tell him. Mrs. Meyers, bring me my purse!"

"Yes, ma'am," she said and hurried off.

"I can't see your face, but I'm assuming you look a little worried about taking money and defying the chief."

He did look that way—sort of embarrassed and nervous and anxious rolled into one.

"This is just going to be our secret—the three of us and Mrs. Meyers. Lizzy, you can keep a secret, can't you?"

"Yes, ma'am."

"And you, Officer Gibson?" she asked.

"I can keep this one, believe me."

"I know Mrs. Meyers can," she said. "And I assure you, you don't get to be my age without having more than a few secrets, so it's agreed."

"Thank you. I'm just so glad you aren't mad at me," he said.

"Mad? Only rabid animals are *mad*. I could be *angry*… but I'm not. Now, if you'll excuse me, I think my dinner is getting cold, and that, young man, is something that I could become angry about. You should also know that it is poor manners to come to somebody's house at dinnertime without an invitation!"

Her stern expression suddenly became a smile, and all the tension left the room.

"Sorry, ma'am, I'm leaving right now!"

"Lizzy, see our guest to the door."

I followed him as he rushed through the curtain and toward the door. He was hurrying to get there as quickly as possible. I opened the door to let him out, and he stopped.

"I forgot about the money. She'll be mad, I mean, angry, if I leave without it, won't she?"

"Probably," I confirmed.

"She's a nice old bird. Not what I expected. I guess lots of things aren't what I expected. Nobody told her about the gun." He said the last word so quietly, I could hardly hear him.

"I don't think Richie even noticed."

"You noticed, but you didn't say anything."

I shrugged.

"Well, I noticed that you saved my bacon. Noticed and locked away," he said, tapping the side of his head. "I won't forget, Betty, Elizabeth Anne, Lizzy."

"Lizzy is all right."

"And David is all right with me. I'm David. I haven't been a cop for long, but it seems like people don't think you have a first name."

He offered his hand, and we shook. "I'm pleased to meet you, Lizzy. I really don't know many people around here. Were you born in Kingston?"

"Born here but raised someplace else. I've only been back a few weeks myself."

"I guess we have a few things in common then. This isn't such a big place that we won't run into each other again."

"I'm sure we will."

"Matter of fact," he said, "I'm going to work hard to keep an eye out for you so we *do* run into each other."

I felt myself blushing. I hoped that Mrs. Meyers would arrive with the money soon.

Fourteen

I SAT ON my little bed and took a sip from my cup of tea. The tea was just the way I liked it: warm and sweet with three heaping spoonfuls of sugar. The cup itself was of fine bone china, made in England, so light it felt like air, so thin I could see light through it. Not the type of cup we'd used at the orphanage, where even the toughest cups had seemed to crack and chip.

The house was quiet and still. Everybody had turned in for the night. I felt cozy and safe, tucked into my little room. For years I'd shared a room with Toni, and while I liked being with her, I'd always fantasized about having a room of my own. Now I wished there was a second little bed here, with Toni tucked into it. Wishing wouldn't make that happen. Nothing would. There was only one thing to do to make her feel closer.

I placed the cup down on the night table and picked up the pad and pen I'd put there. Three times I'd tried to write

Toni, and three times my efforts had ended up crumpled and in the wastebasket in the corner. It wasn't that I didn't want to write to her or didn't have things to say to her, but it was still hard to know what to say. After all, I'd spent more time talking to her than anybody else in my whole life, but I'd never written her a letter before. Could I even be sure that she would get it? I guessed there was only one way to find out, and the starting part was easy enough.

Dear Toni,

I hope this letter finds you well. I also hope it finds you and that this letter-exchange system really works. My train ride was very uneventful. What was waiting for me was a little more eventful. I was picked up by a Rolls-Royce, like I was some kind of movie star. What I really am, of course, is a maid for a very rich family. I knew I was going to be a domestic, but I had no idea just how rich the family would be. That must sound naïve— which you've always accused me of being—because it isn't like poor people have maids, but these people are really, really rich. Probably the richest in Kingston. And, if not the richest, certainly the most influential.

They are also a very nice family. There is the matriarch, Mrs. Remington. She likes classical music, like Mrs. Hazelton does. She is kind and nice, and she likes me. Her oldest son lives in the house. He is different. Not that he isn't nice, but he doesn't really get along well with other people. Perhaps that's not correct. He doesn't really understand people and they don't understand him. He spends a lot of time with his pigeons. There is an older son,

Edward, who lives across town with his family. He is the mayor of Kingston and is very important. He is also very nice, and he actually does look like a movie star.

The people I work with—Mrs. Meyers the housekeeper, James the driver, Nigel the cook and Ralph the gardener—are all nice people. They have worked here so long that they all knew my mother. That is the strangest twist. My mother worked here. I lived here as a child and they all knew me and tell me stories now about what I was like. It's very strange and quite wonderful.

I am writing this as I sit in my room. This is the room my mother lived in before she had me, and then we moved to a guest cottage at the back of the grounds. I grew up right here. Who would have ever thought this was possible? It wasn't a coincidence. Mrs. Remington told me that she had a hand in making it all happen. She is a very important person. So important that even the police chief does what she wants.

Sometimes the things they say to me spark little memories. Mostly, though, it's like I'm being told about somebody I don't know or a movie I haven't watched. Still, it is good to know something after knowing nothing. It makes me feel more...

I struggled for the word that would finish the sentence. I thought of a few before I came up with the right one.

...complete. It feels like a hole inside is being filled up.

When Mrs. Hazelton gave me that envelope, the last thing I wanted was to read what was inside. It hurt to find out about *my past, what had happened to my mother. I guess I need to tell you first.*

This was not going to be easy, but I had to tell her. There was no other way.

I came into the orphanage because my mother was killed. The hard part is that she wasn't killed in a car accident or something like that—she was murdered by my own father. They weren't married, but still, he was my father. He was found guilty and sent away to prison.

It was painful for me to find all of this out. I guess I understand why they'd hide some things, but now I just wonder why they would hide so much from us to begin with. Good or bad, or in this case, even horrible, it is our lives, our past—it's who we are. I'm discovering who I am, and while it's strange and frightening and confusing, it is my journey. It feels like I'm reading a book after living a life that started on chapter four. Now I'm reading something about those early chapters. Maybe my mother wasn't a princess, and there isn't any magic to where I began, but it is my beginning.

I wish you were here to share in it and to help me understand it—the way I'd try to help you with what you're discovering. Toni, I truly miss you. You are my best friend. I know, I know, I can just hear you telling me to stop saying the obvious, but I had to say it. I love you so much.

I'm so sorry that we didn't have the chance to say goodbye. For a while I was angry about it, but you know I can't stay angry at anybody for long, so I certainly couldn't stay mad at you.

I've decided we didn't have a chance to say goodbye because it wasn't really goodbye. It's just until we meet again.

I want you to write back as soon as you can to tell me what you've found out, what's happening in your life, what you're doing, thinking, feeling, and when we can see each other again. Kingston and Toronto aren't close to each other, but they aren't that far apart either. We need to arrange for one of us to come to—

There was a knock on the door.

I pulled the blanket up slightly. "Yes?"

The door opened slowly, and Edward peeked in.

"I'm sorry for disturbing you this late," he said.

"It's all right."

"I saw the light on under your door and hoped you weren't asleep."

"No, I was just writing a letter to a friend." I held it up to show him and then instantly thought better of it, as if he could somehow read the line I'd written about him looking like a movie star.

"May I step in?" he asked.

"Yes, of course."

"I didn't want to wake anybody up, but it's only proper to ask formally before entering the bedroom of a young lady. I wanted to thank you for what you did for my brother today."

"It was nothing, really, nothing," I protested.

"It was much more than that. I heard about the altercation. Things could have gotten out of hand if you hadn't been there to provide a calming influence."

"I really didn't do anything."

"That's not what the officer said."

"You spoke to David—I mean, Officer Gibson?"

"David? It sounds like you spoke to him too," he said.

I felt myself starting to blush for no reason. "When he came to apologize, we spoke for a few seconds."

"He met with both me and the police chief." He chuckled. "I must admit, I felt sorry for him. He seems like a nice young man."

"He is. Well, I think he is."

"Just remember, *seeming* nice doesn't necessarily mean that somebody *is* nice. I only wish I could have convinced your mother of that."

The words seemed to leap out of him, and I saw that he instantly regretted what he'd said. He looked embarrassed. I had to ease the discomfort.

"I wanted to thank you as well," I said.

"Thank me for what?"

"For my mother's headstone. I had no idea it would be so large."

"You have to thank my mother for that."

"I will thank her as well, but Richie told me that you were the one who insisted on it and that you wrote the inscription."

"I wish he hadn't told you any of that," Edward said.

"I'm glad he did. What you wrote was beautiful."

"I didn't write those words as much as feel them. Your mother was a very, very special person. She was a kind and generous soul. She was as close to an angel as I've ever met in my entire life. If only…" He shook his head. "I shouldn't be talking about this. I don't want to cause you any distress."

"If it's about my mother, I'd like to know. There's so much I don't know."

I braced myself for something bad.

He looked like he was thinking, choosing his words carefully.

"Your mother was—how should I say this?—an innocent. She believed in people, and she always saw the best in them."

"My friend Toni says that about me all the time!"

"It's not surprising that you not only look like your mother but are like her inside too. Remarkable. Standing here looking at you, having this conversation in this room, brings me back to a time when I was much, much younger." He shook his head. "I just wish, with all my heart, that I could have convinced her that not all people are worthy of trust."

I knew instantly who he was talking about.

"Because she only saw the good in people, she didn't see the evil. I knew it was there. In the end that's what ended her life. If only she'd listened to me and stayed here—stayed away from him."

There was no longer any doubt. He was talking about the man who had murdered my mother. He was talking about my father.

"That's why I need you to understand that not everything and everyone is the way it seems all of the time. Take that young police officer. Perhaps he is not as nice as he seems.

I want you to take measures to guard yourself, and always be aware. Can you promise me that?"

I nodded.

"Not just with him." He paused again, so long that I almost jumped in to break the awkward silence. "I've been told that you're spending a great deal of time with my brother."

"He tells me stories about my mother and me when I was little. He remembers so much."

"He does absorb facts and recite them, but always be careful of the context of those recollections."

I had no idea what he meant.

"You know that he doesn't understand many social situations, right?"

I nodded.

"That means he might know a date or even a time, but he doesn't know anything about what is behind those facts. For example, have you talked to him about what happened with the police officer?"

"No, I haven't."

"Good. In fact, I recommend that you don't discuss it with him, but if you were to, even years from now, he could tell you the day it happened, who was with him, where he was going, possibly even the license-plate number of the police car. What he couldn't tell you was why he was asked to stop, why he shouldn't have walked away and why that could have led to a significant problem."

"After it happened, he told me that he doesn't talk to strangers."

"And he didn't know the police officer, so he wouldn't talk to him," Edward said. "From Richie's perspective that makes perfect sense. Thank goodness our money and position in the community afford him some protection."

"I didn't expect him to do that with the shovel," I said. "He's always so nice."

"He is basically nice, like a child, but there is a part of that child that is always dangerous. He just doesn't understand the consequences of his actions. I feel bad for saying these things. He is my brother, and I'm very protective of him, but I feel the need to be even more protective of you. I can't ever allow anything to happen to you—to dear Vicki's daughter." He sat down on the edge of my bed. "I just wish I had done more. I wish I could replay what happened. I will never stop feeling that somehow if only..." The words trailed away.

I reached out and put a hand on his hand. "I know you did all that you could."

"You really are your mother's daughter. Here I came to offer you my thanks and comfort, and you've been the one who gave me thanks and comfort."

I didn't know what to answer, but it made me feel warm inside—cared for.

"It's getting late. I must go home before my wife gets worried." He got up and went to the door. "Good night, dear Lizzy."

Fifteen

JAMES AND I stood by the car as Richie opened the cage, took out a bird and spoke a few words to it, so softly that I couldn't hear what he was saying. He then held the bird up and released it, and it fluttered away.

Some of the pigeons flew almost exactly in the direction James said was back to Kingston, back to their coop. Others circled around before going off in that direction, and a couple of them looked like they were going to Kingston by way of the North Pole.

With each release, Richie marked in a notebook the exact time—to the second—when the bird was set free. The race was with dozens of other pigeons being released from locations across the city of Belleville. Now we'd drive and the pigeons would fly the fifty miles back to Kingston. Of course, they'd have a direct route—as the crow flies— and we'd follow the roads. James said there was no question they'd get there first, but Ralph was waiting for them, to mark the exact time of their arrival. Then, as Richie explained it, "Distance divided by time equals speed," and the winning bird would be determined.

With the last pigeon gone, we got into the car, Richie in the back, directly behind James, and me in the front, beside James. He started the engine—it purred like a kitten—and we were off, heading back toward Kingston.

That meant the end of an idea I'd been toying with. We were more than halfway to Hope. I'd fantasized about asking Richie if we could drive there. But really, it wasn't like any of the people I cared for were even there anymore— they were scattered to the winds. Still, there would be lots of people in the town who knew me. Since before I'd climbed on that outbound train, I'd thought about coming back, and what better way than in a Rolls-Royce? I'd just roll down the window, lean out and wave to people on the street, and— well, the whole thing was just silly.

Richie, of course, wouldn't want to go anywhere except back to his pigeons. There was a whole routine involved. Routines were the foundations of Richie's life. There were dozens and dozens of them, and they regulated everything from what foods he ate to what clothing he wore and where he went.

Familiarity made him feel safe. I understood that. Didn't it make everybody and everything seem safer?

In my mind, I'd replayed dozens and dozens of times the conversation I'd had in my room with Edward. The parts about my mother were the most important, but his warning about not trusting anybody—even Richie, maybe especially Richie—had stayed in my head. Mostly Richie was nothing but harmless, almost like a child, but I'd seen a spark of defiance more than just the one time with Officer Gibson. The image of Richie swinging that shovel was burned into my memory. He'd not done anything even close to that since then, but I'd noticed that he became upset when his routines were broken or altered. He didn't do well with change.

I'd thought about how close he was to my mother and me, and I'd begun to realize how hard it would have been for him when we left. If it was hard for Mrs. Remington to understand and accept, it must have been that much harder for Richie.

I'd also thought about David—Officer Gibson. I'd been to town twice since he came to the house. He wasn't the only one keeping an eye out. I was looking for him. I would have died of embarrassment if he or anybody else knew that. But he wasn't much older than me, and was it wrong for me to want some friends my own age?

We continued to drive. Each second was farther from Hope—the home I'd known—and closer to Kingston—the home I was getting to know. I was traveling from past to future—really, from my recent past to both my future and my more distant past. Almost every day I learned more about my life and my mother's life. This was the perfect time, in the car, to see if Richie could tell me even more. I turned around in the seat so I was facing him.

"How often did my mother go with you to the races?"

"She went seventeen times."

I wasn't surprised that he knew the exact number.

"And this is your seventh time," he said.

"I went when I was little?"

Richie went on to talk about the times I'd been out with him. I looked over at James, and he nodded in agreement.

"You always liked my pigeons. I tell them what you told them."

"I don't understand," I said.

"Before they fly away, I tell them what you told them."

I'd noticed him putting the birds close to his face, mumbling something to them, but I'd never made out the words.

"I'm sorry, but I don't remember. What did I say to them? What did you say to them?"

"What I always say to them. 'I love you, little angel.'"

"I don't remember that." But somehow it did seem familiar. Not like something I'd said to the pigeons but like something I'd heard. "It's sweet of you to say that to them."

"It is sweet," James said. "It's also what your mother always said to you, Lizzy."

"She did," Richie said. "You were her little angel."

I kept being stunned again and again by details about my past, and this was so personal, so sweet.

"When you said that to the pigeons the first time, they did really well," Richie said. "They won. That's why I still say it to them."

"Not that they always win," James said. "Maybe next time you should have Lizzy say it to them."

"Would you do that?" Richie asked.

"Of course I would." I'd say to them what my mother had always said to me. I just wished I could remember her voice. Wait—everybody said that I sounded just like her. To hear her voice, all I needed was to hear my voice. But maybe the voice didn't matter as long as I knew the words, what she'd called me—I was her little angel. That made me feel warm inside, like I'd been brought closer to her, and I decided right there that I was going to say those words to my children someday. They would be my angels. All of them.

Richie started to talk about the pigeons and their race results. He listed, race by race, pigeon by pigeon, their times and speeds. These details couldn't possibly be of interest to anybody except other pigeon racers. They were mind numbing, which wasn't the worst possible thing, as it was becoming increasingly hard to turn off my brain at night and go to sleep because of all the new information that kept flowing in.

We moved along Highway 2, the lake to our right. We entered Kingston, and Richie leaned over the front seat. I knew he wasn't interested in conversation but wanted to see the speedometer to make sure that James had slowed down to the speed limit. Of course, James had. I knew that not just because I knew how James drove, but because Richie didn't say anything. If we were traveling too fast he would have mentioned it and insisted that James slow down.

Instead he kept up his running monologue about race results.

I stared out the window. The stores looked vaguely the same as the ones in Hope, but none were familiar to me. I'd been here for almost a month and had only been off the grounds a few times. Mrs. Meyers referred to it as *going to Kingston*. Even though the house was in Kingston, it seemed more like we were on our own little island, almost a separate country or kingdom, surrounded by walls. It was a peaceful kingdom ruled by a kind queen who treated us well.

"There is where your father lives," Richie said.

"What did you say?" I asked, not believing I had heard him correctly.

"He said nothing," James snapped.

"Your father is there," Richie said, pointing out the window.

James let out a big sigh.

"That's where he lives," Richie said.

I looked in the direction he was pointing. A high gray stone wall stretched along the street. What could Richie mean? How could my father...? And then I saw the turrets. At the top of the wall there was barbed wire, and I caught a brief glimpse of a man in one of the turrets. He was wearing a uniform and carrying a rifle. In a flash we passed by a gate and the sign announcing what this place was: *Kingston Penitentiary*.

All the time I'd spent learning about my past, living in the place where we'd lived before my mother's death, I'd been focused on her and on myself. I hadn't even spent a second wondering what had happened to my father—the man who had murdered my mother, the man who had taken her away from me, who had robbed me of not only my mother but also my childhood. And he was there, right behind that wall. Somehow, I'd just assumed he was dead too. And, really, he was. Dead to me.

We continued to drive, the wall to my right soon replaced by shops and houses again. The prison was gone. He was gone. I moved slightly in my seat and there it was again in the side-view mirror—the place where my father lived.

Sixteen

I WALKED OUT the front gate and stopped for a moment to look back, across the perfectly manicured lawn and tended flower beds, at the main house. It looked so beautiful. Like something out of a movie. I'd have to tell Ralph that. He worked so hard. On those grounds were the only people I knew in the whole area—well, except for Edward and Officer Gibson.

I'd hardly set one foot off the grounds since I'd come here. There had been work to do, of course, but I did have time off. It was just that I'd had no place to go and no one to meet. I didn't know the city and I didn't know anybody in it. Back home, the girls and I had sometimes walked around Hope, looking in the shop windows, having ice cream, talking to people we knew, nodding at everyone else. On these streets, I would be alone. Alone wasn't bad. Sometimes I'd sneaked out of the orphanage at night and gone for long walks. They had been calming and reassuring, but part of being reassured was knowing that my bed and my friends and Mrs. Hazelton were all there waiting for me.

I started walking and felt uneasy as the house receded from view and then disappeared completely. I knew where I was going—the bank—and how to get there. Richie had told me in great detail. He had given me the address—178 King Street—and made me repeat both the address and the walking route back to him. I'd almost asked Richie to come with me. I'm sure he would have, but I also knew he didn't like to go into Kingston all that much. I wondered if I should have asked to bring his shovel along with me—as silly as that sounded. There was nothing to fear walking down the main streets of Kingston in broad daylight.

I chuckled at the thought of Officer Gibson pulling up beside me as I marched along with the shovel on my shoulder, and imagined what he'd say to me and what I'd say back to him. Carrying the shovel might have made it more likely that he'd recognize me. Another silly thought, because I was sure he'd know me.

It wasn't just Richie who didn't seem to like leaving the estate. Ralph hardly ever left his gardens. Nigel seemed to go into Kingston just for groceries and only if he couldn't convince Mrs. Meyers to go for him. Mrs. Meyers herself said she had no interest in going except for those occasional shopping trips when she had no choice. She said she was content, and, indeed, she did seem that. She often had a book by her side or shared one with Mrs. Remington, reading out loud to her. Sometimes I'd be dusting or cleaning or polishing within earshot of her reading. It was such a lovely way to spend time.

Mrs. Remington always seemed to stay at home. A few friends visited, as well as Edward, but I didn't think she'd left in the entire time I'd been there. I understood. She had everything she could possibly need right there, and if she didn't have something, she could send somebody else to get it.

The only one who seemed to want to leave was James. He looked for any excuse to drive his car. He said having a car like that and not driving it was like keeping a bird in a cage. I knew that if I asked, he actually would drive me to Hope—assuming he could get permission.

Today I finally had a reason to leave and a place to go. Pressed into my purse were my wages. Each Friday afternoon we all gathered together and stood in a line, waiting to receive our weekly pay packages from Mrs. Remington. In my envelope each week was $35. I now had five weeks' worth of wages, for a total of $175. I still had every cent I'd been paid, because there really was nothing that I needed. My meals were provided, I paid no rent, and I had no expenses. Along with that, I had what was left of the money Mrs. Hazelton had given me. Altogether I had $297.

It was almost impossible to believe I had that much money, but I knew it was true. I'd counted it repeatedly, not because I thought some of it would go missing, but because it was just so amazing to think I had that much. I'd never even *seen* that much money before. Until now, I'd been keeping it in the bottom drawer of my dresser. Mrs. Meyers had finally convinced me—basically ordered me—to open a bank account. It did seem like the proper thing to do, the *grown-up* thing to do.

As I neared the downtown, there was much more activity. There were more cars on the street and more people on the sidewalks. Most of the people passed without giving me a sideways glance when I smiled at them, but others were friendly and nodded and smiled in return or offered a "good morning." Along the street the little shops were coming to life; shades were pulled up and doors opened. Some shoppers were already inside. I stopped in front of a dress store whose mannequins, draped in bright, flowery prints, caught my eye.

I looked down at what I was wearing. Drab, dull colors. Somebody else's clothes, practically the only clothes I owned apart from the two uniforms hanging in the cupboard in my room. Not that I was complaining; many people had less than me. I'd never owned a dress like those in the window. I'd looked at things that fancy in the dress shops in Hope, but there'd never been a reason to go inside. Window-shopping didn't cost money. Toni and I had often stood outside the stores, admiring the clothes on display, talking about what would look good on us, fantasizing about the time when we'd have the money to buy something. Today I had the money.

I straightened my skirt, took a deep breath and opened the door, a little *ding* of the bell above the door announcing I'd arrived.

An hour later I walked back outside. The sun seemed a little brighter. I stopped, put down the bag I was carrying and turned to look at my reflection in the store window. I could hardly believe it was me. One mannequin was now gone; the dress *it* had been wearing, *I* was now wearing. Flowery and feminine, it flowed and fluttered around me as I turned slightly and made a little twirl. It almost looked like I was in the window.

On my feet were new white shoes with a little heel. I'd also purchased a matching white purse. It couldn't really be me reflected in the window. I must be looking at a mannequin or a model in a Simpson's or Eaton's catalog. It certainly didn't look like me. But really, who was I?

Was I Betty or Elizabeth Anne or Lizzy or a little angel? Was I an orphan nobody wanted to adopt? Was I the beloved daughter of a wonderful woman who was a loving mother before her life was taken? Was I the daughter of a murderer, the man who took that life, who destroyed *my* life, who ripped my mother away from me, robbing me of that love?

I looked hard at the reflection, deep into the eyes staring back at me, trying to see behind them—and I knew. I was all of those people. I was defined by where I'd been, but I was something else, something more. I was *me*. I turned away from the reflection, picked up the bag of my old things and continued on my way.

My new purse contained what was left of my money—
not $297.00 but $274.34. Still much more than I'd ever
had before. I'd spent $22.66. I could hardly believe that
I'd allowed myself to do that, but it was as if I'd had no
choice. The dress was perfect and, at $9.00, didn't seem
that expensive—although I'd never owned anything that
cost that much in my life. And I really did need shoes. My
old black ones didn't go with the dress or the season or
my age, for that matter—they were the shoes of an older
woman. Eight dollars for leather shoes was reasonable.
The purse was the finishing touch, and it was on sale for
$5.00—a good price.

I gave my best "good morning" and a big smile to the
first couple who walked past me. They greeted me in an
equally friendly manner. I made a decision right then and
there to give everybody a smile. This wasn't Hope, but there
was no reason to believe that people here weren't just as
friendly, just as nice. Besides, how could I not smile? I felt
so happy that I had to fight the urge to skip instead of walk.
I felt so good, so light, so, well…pretty. When I did return
to Hope, when I did see Toni and the other girls again, I'd be
wearing this exact outfit.

Deep in my thoughts, I lost count of the number of
streets I'd passed—Richie had given me an exact number—
but I knew the bank couldn't be more than a few blocks
ahead. Maybe I'd even pass by another dress store and
go inside. Not that I'd buy anything, but I could browse.
If only Toni were with me. It would have been so much fun

trying on clothes, spending time with her, giggling at things only we found funny, making quiet little comments about people we passed. Toni had a way of making me laugh.

I noticed that one side of the road was no longer filled with stores. Instead, there was the high cement wall of the prison. The prison that held the man who had killed my mother. I wanted to look away, I wanted to run away, but I couldn't. I felt like it was calling out to me, like I was being drawn toward it.

I turned to cross the street and jumped back as a car horn blared and a car zoomed by me, so close that the breeze blew my dress. My heart raced, not just from the close call but from my closeness to the wall. I took a deep breath and steadied myself as I waited for a gap in the traffic. I moved gingerly across the street, the straps of my new shoes digging into the backs of my feet.

I was now in the shadow cast by the wall. It towered above me, blocking out not only the sun but also, it seemed, the sky itself. It was much cooler in the shade, and I had the peculiar feeling that I'd been captured by the wall. Then again, perhaps the chill had less to do with the shade and more to do with how I was feeling. I was scared.

As I walked, I reached out and touched the wall. It was rough and cold against my hand. I knew it had to be very thick. As I moved, I looked straight ahead, only giving the wall a sideways glance.

I came up to the gate, and now I could see through the metal bars and beyond. There really wasn't much to see—just stone buildings behind a small courtyard. In the distance, a man walked across the space. For a split second a surge of electricity rushed through me—*Is that him?*—until I realized he was in uniform. He was a guard, and within a few more strides, even he was gone. I waited, hoping that somebody else would appear, but nobody did. If I hadn't seen that one person, it would have seemed like the whole place was deserted.

"Can I help you?"

I jumped at the sound of the voice—male and gruff. Another man dressed in uniform had stepped out of a little doorway to the side of the gate.

"Can I help you?" he asked again. This time his voice was a little softer, but I still didn't know what to say. "Are you here for a visitation?"

"Visitation?"

"To visit one of the prisoners?"

My mind raced. I should just say no and turn and run away, but I didn't.

"Gordon Sullivan," I said.

He looked surprised. "Gord doesn't get many visitors."

"You know him?"

"I know everybody in here, especially the long-termers. Go over there and sign in."

He pointed at a doorway beside the gate.

"You're late, but there's a small chance you can still get in, but you have to hurry."

I jumped forward, thanking him, stumbling in my new shoes. I longed for my old comfortable shoes. I came up to the door, hesitated again, then opened it and stepped inside. I was in a small office, empty except for a uniformed officer standing behind a counter. He scowled at me. I smiled timidly, and his scowl seemed to grow.

"I'm here for visitation."

"Then you should have arrived on time," he snapped. "Everybody else has already left."

"I'm sorry. I didn't know." I started to turn away.

"So stop wasting my time and sign in." He shoved a piece of paper and a pen across the counter at me.

I took them and started to read. There were three simple lines to fill out:

Name of prisoner to be visited:

Name of visitor:

Relationship to prisoner:

I filled in the first two lines, listing my name as Elizabeth Anne Roberts, and hesitated on the third. Should I say *daughter*? Finally, I put *relative*. That was enough. I handed him back the form.

"Through that door," he said without even glancing at the form. "Follow the yellow line on the floor until you reach the next officer."

"Thank you. Thank you for letting me in."

"Just don't expect to get in again if you come late."

I went through a door and down a hall, the yellow line in the middle of the floor my guide. Up ahead was another door. I went to open it, and it was locked. I looked down at the floor. The line led right up and under the door and through a small wired window. I could see that it continued on the other side. There was a buzzing sound. I pushed the door again, and it opened. On the other side was another counter, this time with two guards behind it.

"You're late," one of them said.

"The guard out front said it was okay for me to come," I said.

"It's not a problem for us," the other guard said. "We're just surprised. Stan doesn't let in anybody who's late. He must have liked you."

The other guard laughed. "Stan doesn't like anybody, so this must be a first." He put a big plastic basket up on the counter. "Put all your things in here."

"Everything?" I asked.

"Nothing can be brought in. Nothing can be given to the prisoner," he said.

"I wouldn't give him anything, it's just that…" I thought about leaving my new purse, with all that money in it, unattended.

"Don't worry," he said, reading my concern. "Everything is locked up. The only people you have to worry about are on the other side of the bars."

I placed my new purse in the basket. I couldn't believe how attached I felt to it already. On top I placed the bag containing my old clothing, shoes and purse. It was like a layer of protection for the things that mattered.

"Is this your first time here?" one of them asked.

"Yes."

"I thought so. I would have remembered you. I'll bring you the rest of the way. All the other visitors have already passed by."

He circled around the counter and held open a door for me and then came in after me. For the first time I noticed that he had a long, large black club attached to his belt. It looked threatening.

"You aren't carrying any weapons, drugs or contraband, are you?" he asked.

"Of course not!" I exclaimed. Although I didn't even know what contraband was, I knew I wasn't carrying anything.

"Standard question that has to be asked," he said. "Strange though. Would anybody carrying something illegal answer truthfully when we ask?"

"I don't know."

"Let me explain the procedure. You're going to be seated on one side of a table and the prisoner on the other. Between you is a wooden divider about a foot high. You are forbidden to reach over it or make any contact with the prisoner."

That was actually reassuring.

"If there is any trouble, you simply have to call out and a guard will intervene."

"What sort of trouble?" I no longer felt reassured.

"I've seen all sorts of circuses erupt in there. We've had to separate prisoners from adjoining tables and had brawls between the prisoners and their wives or girlfriends."

"The prisoners attacked them?"

"Often it's the other way around. We don't cater to the best or most refined clientele around here—no offense."

Was he talking about me? I was the clientele, here to visit a prisoner?

"The other visitors have already been brought down. Visiting time has already begun, so you know you won't have as much time as you normally would."

"That's all right."

It was better than all right. I didn't know what I was going to say to him to begin with, so short would be better. I just wanted to lay eyes on him, the man who had done this terrible thing. I wanted to see him, maybe tell him what I thought of him, what he'd cost me.

"Who are you here to visit?" he asked.

"Gordon Sullivan."

"Gordie?" He sounded genuinely surprised. "He doesn't get many visitors, not since his mother died."

That was my grandmother—the mother of the man who killed my mother.

"How do you know Gordie?"

I was going to say "relative," but I didn't. "I'm his daughter."

"You're the little girl who was left behind?"

"Did he talk to you about me?"

"Not a word," he said.

"But how did you know?"

"There wasn't anybody in Kingston who didn't follow the trial in the papers. The court gallery was crowded every day. A murder like that is pretty big news."

A murder. My mother. And my father did it. The man I was going to visit right now. If I had had the strength, I would have told the guard I had changed my mind and demand to be taken back out to the street, but I didn't.

"Does Gordie know you're coming today?"

"No, he doesn't." Up until a few minutes ago, I didn't know myself.

"Then this is going to be a big surprise. Hopefully, a good one for both of you."

He led me into a big room. There were dozens of people seated at tables. On the far side of the tables were the prisoners, all dressed in bright orange coveralls. On the side closest to us were the visitors. Mostly they were women, and there were children sitting beside their mothers or grandmothers.

He led me to a table, one of only three that were unoccupied. "Take a seat. He's being brought down from the cell block right now."

"Thank you."

"Gordie, your father...he's not a bad guy."

"He killed my mother," I said, surprised by the words.

"Yeah, I know. I meant for here," he said, sweeping his arm around the room. "He doesn't cause nobody any grief, keeps to himself, follows the rules."

It was nice to know he was a well-behaved murderer.

"Have a good visit," he said and left.

I looked around the room without being too obvious. I noticed almost immediately that guards ringed the room.

They all were in uniform, hats on their heads, with clubs at their sides. Some were holding on to their clubs; one guard was spinning his around like it was a baton and he the drum major.

There were two guards in the corner who had more than clubs. They had guns. One had a revolver in a holster on his belt, like a police officer, and the second held a rifle. He had his back to the wall and was scanning the room slowly.

The room was filled with voices. I couldn't help but overhear the conversation to my right. A woman with two children was telling the prisoner how the kids were doing in school. It was as if they were sitting around the kitchen table, having lunch together, having a regular conversation. He seemed really interested in how they were doing, and the whole thing, them talking to him, seemed oddly familiar to me.

Other voices not as pleasant or friendly also rose up. It sounded like there was a serious argument going on a few tables away. I looked over and the prisoner, who happened to be looking in my direction, gave me a threatening scowl. I quickly looked away, casting my eyes on the table in front of me.

"Oh my god. Lizzy…it's you, isn't it?"

I looked up. On the other side of the table stood a large man in orange prison clothing.

"It's me," I said, my voice just a whisper.

He burst into tears. I didn't know what I'd expected, but this wasn't it.

He slumped down, taking the seat on the opposite side of the table. "They told me somebody was here to visit me, but they didn't tell me it was my daughter. Oh my god, my good god."

Mrs. Hazelton would have lectured him for taking the Lord's name in vain, and for an instant I almost did the same.

"It's like looking at your mother." He rubbed his eyes with the back of his hand. "It's unbelievable how much you look like her."

"People tell me that."

"It's like I'm looking at her. The same but different." He smiled—a sad little smile. "Do you know how long I've prayed for this moment? You've been in my prayers each night."

Prayers? Did murderers think God listened to them?

"I prayed that you'd be well cared for, that the people who adopted you would be good people."

"I was never adopted."

"But they promised me you would be. They said that if my mother didn't pursue custody, they had a really good family for you—a better family."

I shook my head. "I grew up in an orphanage in Hope."

"They promised. I don't know why I thought they'd keep that promise. It was just that my mother, you know, she did her best, but she had problems with the bottle. She lived inside of it. I wanted better for you than what I'd had. If I'd only known! Even my mother would have been better than an orphanage."

"They treated me well!" I exclaimed. "Mrs. Hazelton and the staff were good people, and they always—"

"I'm sorry," he said, cutting me off. "I didn't mean to say anything against people I don't know. It looks like they did a good job."

I was suddenly grateful that I was wearing my new dress. It felt wrong, but I wanted to impress him.

"I feel so bad," he said. "I always thought you'd grow up in a family, with people who would care for you like you were their own."

That had been my fantasy too.

"You gotta understand, all we have here is time, and I've spent a lot of it thinking about you, about you being cared for right. If I'd known they were just going to dump you in some orphanage, we would have fought for you. My mother would have applied for custody."

"I wasn't dumped," I said. "Mrs. Hazelton was like a mother, and the girls were like my sisters."

"That makes me feel better." He paused. "It's bad enough what those people did to me, taking away the woman and daughter that I loved, but it helped to think that at least your life was saved."

"Those people?" I asked.

"The police, the judge, the jury. All of those people."

I felt a rush of rage surge through me. "Maybe those people wouldn't have done that to you if you hadn't murdered my mother!" I snapped back loudly.

I felt people turn and stare. His face showed no reaction. Not anger, not guilt, not remorse. Nothing.

"I was convicted of killing your mother. That doesn't mean I did it."

"Are you saying you're innocent?" I demanded. The force of my words shocked me.

"I was going to ask you what you know about what happened, but obviously you know some things."

"I know everything. I read the newspaper reports. I know that you murdered my mother!"

He didn't answer right away. His face was like a mask, not revealing anything. Finally he spoke.

"I did a lot of things, things I regret, but the one thing I didn't do was kill Vicki. I loved your mother with all my heart. As much as I loved—*still* love—you."

His words took my breath away.

"How long have you known?" he asked.

"A few weeks. They told me when I left the orphanage. They gave me information about my past even though they weren't supposed to. I came back to live in Kingston."

"And you decided to visit me, thinking that I'd murdered your mother."

"You were convicted," I snapped.

He waved his hand around the room. "They say that everybody in jail tells you they're innocent. Most aren't. Some of us are. Being convicted of something doesn't mean you did it."

"Then what does it mean?" I demanded.

"Maybe it means that you had a bad lawyer or didn't have the right connections or were dirt poor. There are no rich people in prison." He paused. "Or maybe it means you were framed."

"And you're telling me you were framed?"

"It doesn't matter what I say. It's just a fact. A fact that makes it even worse. I'm here, convicted of a crime I didn't commit. The man who really did murder your mother is still out there, free, and I'm here, locked up like a dog. No, not like a dog. Nobody would treat a dog the way they treat us. We're not just less than human—we're less than animals."

We stared at each other, as if neither of us could come up with the words that needed to be said next.

"But none of that matters. Today, you're here. Seeing that you're alive and doing okay, well, that just makes the last thirteen years seem better. It doesn't matter what happened to me because you're here now."

"How long before you're free?"

"In three years I'll have served two-thirds of my time. Technically, I'll be eligible for parole."

A chill went up my spine. That wasn't that long. As long as he was inside, I was safe.

"But that's not going to happen. They're not going to let me out of here."

"They?" I asked.

"It's not just what the judge recommended at the sentencing. The same people who put me in here are going to make sure I don't go anywhere until my full time is served. I'll be here for another twelve years—the full twenty-five." He shook his head. "They took away the woman I loved, and they'll have taken away twenty-five years of my life, but that doesn't matter. You returned. My little angel has returned."

"That's what my mother called me."

He laughed. "That's what I called you, and then she started calling you that. I always said she was an angel sent down from heaven and you, well, you were my little angel."

I put my hands to my mouth to stop myself from speaking. I didn't remember my mother ever saying those words to me, but I *did* remember a male voice calling me his little angel. Was it his voice?

"Time!" a man called out. "Visiting time is over!"

"It can't be time," my father said. "There's so much I need to ask you about your life, about what happened, about *you*. You have to promise me you'll come back next week for visiting day. You have to promise!"

I didn't have to think. "I'll be back. I promise."

"Lizzy, thank you, and I love you, my little angel."

Seventeen

I LEFT THE prison in a fog. I stood there on the street, looking back at the gate. Had I really been inside? Had I really spoken to my father? It was like a dream.

I had to focus and remember where I was and where I was going. The bank. I was going to the bank. I turned to my right and started walking, with the wall of the prison as my guide. Behind that wall I could now picture the man who was my father—Gordon Sullivan. He was no longer just a name on a page, but a real person. But what did that mean? Would I really go back and see him again? Would I, the once-lost daughter, visit him faithfully from now until he was released? Or was even this single visit disloyal to the memory of my mother? He'd called me his little angel, he'd told me he loved me, he'd told me he was innocent. Could that be possible? If he *was* innocent, then not only my mother's life but also mine and his had been taken away. It meant that the real killer had never been brought to justice, and he was still out there somewhere.

A chill went through my body and I looked all around, as if the real killer was watching me, following me, and was ready to strike again, to kill the daughter of the woman he'd killed. There were people on the other side of the street—a mother and her two children. She wasn't the killer, but there were other people up ahead and—

My heel caught and I tumbled forward, crying out as my knees slammed into the pavement and my purse and bag flew out of my hands. More embarrassed than hurt, I scrambled to my feet and grabbed my things, and then I realized that my left knee hurt. I looked down. It was bleeding. Worse, there was a rip in my new dress! I slumped down and sat on the curb. I hiked up my dress slightly so it wouldn't get stained with blood. My mind was spinning, trying to figure out what I could do next, and only one answer came: I burst into tears.

Cars whizzed by in front of me, and I knew there were people walking by. I needed to regain my composure, but I couldn't. There was nothing I could do to stop the tears, and nobody who could help me. It wasn't like I had a mother to hold me and make me feel better. Not even a Mrs. Hazelton to take care of the wound. Not a single friend to seek comfort from. Only a prisoner father who was locked away behind those walls. I was alone, sitting on the curb in a strange town, with a bleeding knee and a torn new dress. Of all of these things, the torn dress bothered me the most.

Big, deep sobs started in my chest and heaved up and out. I couldn't contain them, and I buried my face in my hands.

"Are you all right?" a woman's voice asked.

I looked up at the woman.

"I'm fine," I sobbed and then buried my face in my hands again. I heard her walk away. What did it matter? There was nothing she could do to change anything.

Then I heard a car slow down and come to a stop. It parked so close to me that I could feel the heat from the engine. I didn't know who it was or what he wanted, but I had to get up and away.

"I told you I'd see you around."

I looked up. Officer Gibson—David—was standing over me.

"Strange. I've only talked to you three times, and two of those times you've been crying," he said. "Is it me?"

I tried to say something but instead just sobbed louder. He bent down so that he was at my level. "Your knee is cut."

I nodded my head, but no words came out.

"Let's start by fixing that up," he said.

He took me by the hand and helped me to my feet. Then he slipped an arm around my waist to steady me. I did feel unsure on my feet. He brought me around to the side of the car, opened the back door and sat me down on the seat, my legs still outside the car. He reached through the open window of the front seat and pulled out a first-aid kit.

He kneeled down in front of me. "It doesn't look too bad. It's not going to need stitches or anything. I'm just going to clean it off first." He took a ball of cotton and poured some liquid onto it. "This might hurt a bit."

He pressed it down and I had to fight the urge to jerk away from the sting. He dabbed it a few times.

"Now we'll cover it up." He pulled out a large bandage and then did something that surprised me. He bent in closer and blew on the cut. "I'm drying it so the bandage will stick." He carefully put the bandage over the scrape and patted the edges to hold it down.

"Thank you," I said. "Thank you very much."

"So what exactly happened?"

"I tripped and fell."

"That could happen to anybody. And where were you off to, all dressed up so fancy? You aren't late for a date, are you?"

"No!"

"Because I don't want to be fighting some jealous boyfriend who sees me on bended knee in front of you and thinks I'm proposing marriage to you."

"I don't have a boyfriend!" I exclaimed. "I was just on my way to the bank to open an account."

"A bank account? Am I to assume you have a fortune in that purse?" he said, tapping it with a finger.

"I have enough money to open an account." To me it was a fortune.

"In that case I have no choice. It's my duty to provide an armed guard to take you to the bank."

"I'll be okay. Honestly."

"Are you trying to get me in trouble again?" he asked.

"Of course not...how would you get in trouble?"

"To allow you to come to harm would be dereliction of duty. Can you imagine how much trouble I'd be in if I allowed you to go on your own and you were robbed? I might be relieved of duty, stripped of uniform and deported from Kingston."

I now realized he was joking.

"And judging from your expression, you think I'm joking," he said. "But believe me, I'm not going to risk getting the chief of police and mayor of Kingston mad at me again. Now, into the front seat, please."

He offered me his hand and I stood up. He opened the front door and helped me inside, closing the door behind me. Then he circled around and climbed behind the wheel.

"Do you think I should put on the siren?" he asked.

"No, of course—you're joking again, right?"

"I am, but if you asked, I *would* put the siren on."

We pulled away from the curb, and he said, "You don't have to answer if you don't want to, but you weren't crying because of your knee, were you?"

"Not the knee." Not even the dress being torn. "I just met my father."

"And he said something that made you cry?"

"He didn't say anything wrong. It's really hard to explain."

"I've been told I'm a good listener. Is your father being here part of the reason you moved back to Kingston?"

"I didn't even know he lived here until yesterday."

"And he lives right around here?"

I didn't know how much he knew or what I was supposed to say. I was going to find out if he really was a good listener. "My father is an inmate in the Kingston Penitentiary."

"I'm so sorry to hear that."

I tried to judge what he was thinking from his voice or his expression, but there was no hint.

"That must be very hard. How long is he in for?"

"He was sentenced to twenty-five years."

"There aren't many crimes that draw that long a sentence." He paused. "In fact, I know of only one."

He pulled the car into the parking lot of the bank and we came to a stop.

"Do you know anything about me?" I asked.

"I know that you're a very kind, very pretty young woman who works for the Remington family. I know that you seem to cry a lot, and I know you saved my job by not saying anything about the gun. Is there more I should know?"

"Probably a lot."

In a quick burst I told him about my father's conviction for murdering my mother. About living my life in the orphanage and about coming back here only a few weeks ago after finding out those things myself. The entire story rushed out fast, and I was surprised by how open I was being.

"I'd never met my father before today," I said. "I was too little to remember him."

"Then I can understand why you're so upset. None of this has been easy on you, and meeting him there—well, a prison visit must have been hard."

"I don't even know what I'm supposed to do now. He told me he loved me, and he told me that he is innocent, that he didn't do it."

"Everybody in jail says they're innocent."

"That's what he said."

"Just because it's said doesn't mean it's not true. Innocent people can be convicted. How much do you know about the trial, the evidence against him?"

"Not much. Just what the newspaper articles said."

"If you'd like, I can ask some questions, do a little digging, maybe even look into the case files," he offered.

"You can do that?"

"This is a real police uniform, you know."

I laughed, and he laughed with me.

"But I have to be honest: you may not like what I find out. Are you going to be all right with that? Me telling you the truth?"

"The truth shall set you free," I said.

"But not your father. It may only provide you with proof that he committed the crime he was convicted of."

"I'd rather know that. I would."

"Then I'll look. Why don't you go into the bank and open your account? I'll wait here for you."

"You don't have to wait."

"I don't have to, but I'm going to wait anyway. I can't expect a girl with such a serious injury to practically limp across town on one good leg."

I didn't want to argue. It would be nice to be driven, nice not to walk. Nice to be with him.

"Thank you."

"I have to warn you, though, that if I get a radio call I might have to leave, and I don't want you to think I just abandoned you."

"I'll be as quick as I can."

Eighteen

HALF AN HOUR later, most of the money was gone from my purse. It felt lighter. I felt lighter. In its place was a small passbook, listing my name, an account number and the amount in my account: $250.00. I'd kept $24.34 out of the account. I wasn't going to get paid for a few more days, and while there was absolutely nothing I needed to spend money on, it felt good to have a little bit with me.

I was happy to see that David and his car were still there. He opened the passenger door and gracefully bowed and gestured with one hand for me to enter. If it weren't for the lights on the roof and the writing on the side of the vehicle, the uniform he was wearing and the gun strapped to his side, it would have been like a date. I climbed in.

"So would you like me to drive you home?" he asked.

Home—where was home? Was it back in Hope at an orphanage that was nothing more than a pile of burned timbers? Was it the guest cottage at the back of the

Remington estate? Was it the little room I now slept in? No, it was someplace else.

"Can you drive me to the corner of Charles and Montreal?" I asked.

"I can drive you anywhere you want."

We started driving. There were some staticky voices on the radio. I couldn't really make out what was being said, but there were lots of numbers thrown in.

"Do you dance?" David asked.

"Everybody can dance."

"Not according to my sisters. They say I have two very large left feet. I guess that isn't the best way to convince you to go out on a date with me."

"You're asking me out?"

"That was the dance question. Would you be interested in accompanying me to a dance next Saturday?"

"I've never been to a dance before." And the only thing I might have worn he'd now seen—plus it was ripped.

"Then this would be your chance. Just think—even if you didn't want to go with me, you'd still be at a dance. So?"

I nodded. "I'd like that." Maybe I'd have to buy something else after all.

"Then it's a date! The dance starts at eight, so I'll pick you up at seven thirty, although I can't promise you as fancy a ride as this. My car doesn't have a siren."

He pulled the car over to the side of the road. "So here we are, the corner of Charles and Montreal. Why are we here? Do you want to go to church?"

On one of the four corners sat a big church. Unfortunately, that still left three corners. "Not to church. To my home."

"I thought you lived at the Remington mansion."

"I live there now, but I lived here before, with my mother."

"Really? Which house?"

That was the difficult question. "I'm not sure. I was hoping it would come back to me, but it hasn't."

"Then allow me to help. After all, I am a police officer, so a little detective work might do the trick. First off, do you remember if your house had a lot of seats, a bell and an altar at the front?"

"Not that I recall."

"Then we can eliminate the church. Second, was your mother well off?"

"She worked as a maid at the Remington home, just like me. So...no."

"Then we can probably eliminate the house on the southwest corner as well, since it looks a little out of her price range—and mine for that matter. Look at the other two—does anything look familiar?"

I looked at one and then the other. "I'm not sure."

"If you had to make a guess, which would you choose?"

I looked again. "That one. I'm not sure why—I just have a feeling."

"Good enough for me. Let's go see it." He got out of the car, and before I could object, he was at my side, opening the door for me, extending a hand to help me out.

"I just wanted to see it," I said.

"We need to get closer. That might twig some more memories. How old were you when you left here?"

"Almost four."

"Then we better get really close." He led and I followed, right to the front of the house and then down the walk and onto the porch.

"What are you doing?" I asked.

"I'm going to knock on the door and ask if you can go inside. At three, you probably spent all your time inside the house or in the backyard, so the front wouldn't be that familiar."

"The backyard. I think I spent time there."

"Good. That's where we'll go once we have permission."

He knocked on the door loud and hard. We waited, but there was no answer. He knocked again, even louder, but still there was no reply.

"Nobody's home, so I guess we'll just have to let ourselves into the backyard," he said.

"Should we do that?"

"Why not? If somebody calls the police, I'll already be here."

He led me off the porch and around the side. Our way was blocked by a high wooden fence. He gave it a push. It was locked. He reached over the gate and fumbled around, and there was a click. The gate swung open.

"Ladies first."

If going to the prison to visit my father was a mistake, this could be a bigger one.

"Come on—don't worry," he said.

Now it seemed like I had no choice. I walked through the gate and readied myself for some awful wave of memory to overwhelm me, but I felt nothing. It was just a yard: grass in the center and flower beds along the back, but it didn't seem familiar to me at all. So much could have changed in thirteen years. Or maybe I'd guessed wrong, and this wasn't even the right house. Even if it was, we hadn't lived there long, and I had been very young.

"So does it look familiar, bring back some happy memories for you?" David asked.

"No memories—nothing. This might not be the right house."

"Okay, let's knock on the door of the other house."

"No, I don't want to put you to any more trouble. This probably is it, but I can't remember anything—" I stopped. There, at the back of the house, was a place where the brick was chipped away, and suddenly I remembered. That's where my mother had fallen to the ground. That's where I was when everybody came. I closed my eyes and looked away, but the image was still in my head.

My head started spinning, and then everything went black.

ᘓ

I startled awake, looked around and saw David staring down at me. He looked worried. I was lying in the backseat of the police car.

"Drink this," he said, handing me a Thermos.

"What is it?" I asked. My mouth felt like it was filled with cotton wool.

"Coffee. Take a sip."

I didn't like coffee, but I took a little swig. "What happened?"

"You fainted. I caught you on the way down, or you would have had more than a scraped knee."

I tried to get up, and he put a hand on my shoulder. "You're not getting up yet. I only guarantee catching you the first time."

"I'm fine."

"Fainting is nature's way of saying you're not so fine. Have you had enough to eat today?"

"I ate breakfast. It's not that. It's just...just..."

"Just what?"

"That backyard. That was where my mother was... was...that's where they found her. And me."

He let out a big sigh. "Did you wake up today wondering how you could make this the most difficult day possible?"

"It wasn't all bad. I bought a new dress."

"And it's torn."

"I met my father."

"In prison," he said. "And then you visited the house where the worst thing in your entire life happened. What wasn't so bad about today?"

"I got asked out to the first dance of my life." I thought about what he must think of me now and added, "If you still want to take me."

"Are you kidding? If the last hour is any indication of what life is like with you, I can't even *imagine* the excitement that awaits me. But for now, I better get you home."

"I can walk if it's too much trouble," I said.

"There was no way I was going to let you walk home *before* you fainted, so now it's out of the question. Besides, it's not any trouble. It's a pleasure."

Nineteen

I CARRIED THE tray holding afternoon tea. Mrs. Remington was sitting in her favorite seat by the window in the parlor, sunshine streaming in on her. She said that she was like a cat and nothing made her happier than sitting in the sun.

Mrs. Meyers sat across from her, reading out loud. It was part of their afternoon routine. She read to her, they had tea together, and then they discussed what she'd read. Routine was very important in this house.

I'd already been out to take Richie his tea. He didn't seem too interested though. One of his pigeons wasn't well, and he was fretting over it, trying to nurse it back to health. He'd hardly even noticed I was there and had only said a few words about his bird, nothing else. Not even a greeting or a goodbye or a thank-you.

"Is that Lizzy?" Mrs. Remington asked.

"Yes, ma'am."

"I thought it had to be from the lightness of your footsteps. Other people I can tell by the noise they make, but with you it's the noise you *don't* make that gives you away."

I poured a cup for both Mrs. Remington and Mrs. Meyers and then added two cubes of sugar to each. I knew that Mrs. Remington often snuck in a third cube, but she didn't like to admit it.

"Lizzy, come and join me. Have a seat." She patted the chair beside her, and I sat down.

"And perhaps, Mrs. Meyers, you could go and get some of those chocolate biscuits I like so much but never have with my afternoon tea."

"I can go," I offered.

"No. I'd like you to stay so that we can chat."

I looked at Mrs. Meyers. She shrugged to indicate she didn't know what was going on. Mrs. Remington waited until her footsteps had receded and then faded to nothing.

"Mrs. Meyers told me that you opened a bank account."

"Yes, ma'am."

"The largest of oaks begins with the smallest of acorns. I was also told that due to the fire you were unable to finish your school year."

"Mrs. Hazelton is hoping to arrange for me to get my graduation diploma."

"But so far it hasn't arrived. And if she can't?"

I hadn't allowed myself to even think about that, but now the question was before me. "Then I'll take some correspondence courses through the mail."

"Excellent. And then?"

"I had thought before about becoming a nurse."

"And has something happened to change your mind?" she asked.

"No, it's just that it's two years and a lot of money and—"

"Money is not a problem if the will is strong. There is a nursing school associated with Kingston General Hospital. It is a well-respected program, and I know the chair of the board of directors and the president of the hospital. I might have some influence."

"That would be wonderful. Thank you, ma'am."

"You need to work hard and continue to save, and perhaps I can be of some assistance. There was one other thing I wanted to talk to you about."

"Yes, ma'am."

"This is more delicate. Lizzy, give me your hand."

I reached out, and she took my hand in both of hers. What was she going to say now?

"I was told that you made a visit yesterday to your father in the penitentiary," she said.

"Yes, I did...but how did you know?" I hadn't told anybody except David.

"Kingston may seem like a big city to you, but in many ways it is not much different than a village, and there isn't much that goes on that I don't become aware of. I suppose I understand why you went. You must have been curious to lay eyes on the man who killed your mother."

"It wasn't something I set out to do. Richie mentioned he was there, and then I was walking by, and it was almost like an accident."

"People get hurt in accidents, even killed. Lizzy, I want you to know that I have nothing but your best interests at heart. You need to seriously consider whether or not you want to go back."

"You don't think I should?" I asked. I had been struggling with my promise to return.

"It's not my decision to make. But I think it's better to look toward the future instead of the past. For example, you must be looking forward to going to that dance this Saturday."

I was shocked that she knew about that as well.

"I told you there's not much that goes on that I don't hear about, although I just broke my promise to Mrs. Meyers that I wouldn't say anything."

"That may be the last bit of gossip I tell you," Mrs. Meyers said as she returned with a plate of cookies.

"I'm sorry for breaking your confidence, my dear, but I envy our Lizzy so much. Going out dancing on a Saturday night with a handsome young man," Mrs. Remington said.

"That would be better than playing gin rummy with Nigel and James in the kitchen," Mrs. Meyers said.

"So that's what you do down there," Mrs. Remington said.

"I thought you'd know that, since you claim to know everything already."

"Not everything but certainly a lot. In the case of Lizzy's visit to the prison, the superintendent of the prison sings in the same church choir as the chief of police and gave him a call to mention it. He, in turn, told Edward, who called me."

That explained how she knew. It also made it clear that if I did decide to go back, she'd know that too.

"And Lizzy, do you have the proper clothing for a dance, something to catch this young man's eye?" Mrs. Remington asked.

"I have some new shoes and a new dress," I said. Mrs. Meyers had already repaired the rip in my new dress so expertly that even I couldn't tell where it had been. "Although I'm not sure it's the proper thing for a dance."

"Mrs. Meyers, you are a wizard with needle and thread. Is there something around here, something that hasn't been worn for a while, that you could transform into a dress suitable for a dance?"

"I'm sure I could find a thing or two," Mrs. Meyers said.

"Then it's settled. Our Lizzy is going out, and we'll promise not to ask her for too many details." She gave my hand a big squeeze. "Even if the past is dark, the future is bright. Let's help you move forward."

"Yes, ma'am."

I was going to move forward, but that didn't mean I couldn't still look over my shoulder as I moved.

Twenty

"SEE IF YOU can coax him into eating something,"
Mrs. Meyers said as she handed me the tray. "He hasn't
eaten since breakfast yesterday."

Richie had been in the pigeon coop all of the previous
day and then had refused to go back to the house to sleep.
Nigel and Ralph had put a little cot in the coop. He was
so worried about his sick bird. It was both peculiar and
touching that he cared so much for them. He was such
an unusual combination of things that I had to admit
I felt protective of him, and I thought perhaps I could
convince him to leave the coop. I also had an ace or two up
my sleeve.

"Do you want me to come out with you?" Mrs. Meyers
asked.

"I'll be fine."

"You know he doesn't do as well when his routine has
been changed," she said.

"I know, but I understand. He really does care for those birds."

She laughed. "Possibly more than he cares for anything or anybody else."

"Mrs. Hazelton told me that you can usually judge a person by the way he treats animals. Somebody who is kind to animals is usually kind to people. Somebody who would kick a dog would probably kick a person, she always told us."

"Richie is kind, but you have to remember he's a whole different kettle of fish." She looked worried, and I got the feeling that the worried look had less to do with Richie and more with me. "I'm going to come out with you—not into the coop, but I'll be right outside if you need me."

Her offer was reassuring and worrying all at once, but I wasn't going to tell her not to come. We walked out the back door and across the grounds toward the coop.

"I'm almost finished with your dress," Mrs. Meyers said. "I think I'm only one more fitting away from it being done."

Mrs. Meyers was making me a new dress from some material she'd salvaged from an old dress of Mrs. Remington's. She really was a wizard with a sewing machine.

"Thanks so much for all the work you're doing," I said.

"It's been a pleasure. We're just a bunch of old fogies around here. Having you here has been a breath of fresh air. Your mother was a very good seamstress. She made almost all of your clothes."

"I didn't know that." There was so much I didn't know.

"If you'd like, I could teach you how to sew, so that you can make your own outfits."

"I'd like that very much."

"Your mother and I used to spend time in the kitchen sewing—I taught her a few things. We'd work and chat and drink tea. You and I could do the same."

"That would be wonderful!"

"It will be my pleasure. Sitting and sewing with your mother was one of the many things I missed when the two of you moved out."

I saw the opening I'd been looking for. "Why did we move out?"

"*Perhaps* your mother wanted to strike out on her own. *Perhaps* it was just time. I don't know for certain. Shall we do the fitting tonight?"

There was something odd about the way she said *perhaps*, and the way, once again, that she changed the subject when I asked about our leaving. Of course, her response made me want to know more. Was something being hidden from me?

Mrs. Meyers stopped at the door to the coop. "I'll be right out here." She walked over and sat down on a bench to take in the morning sun.

I tapped on the door of the coop and then entered. Richie was sitting in the corner, his back to me. A pigeon was on his right shoulder. Was the sick bird feeling better? No, this was a gold collar, and the sick one was a fancy. I'd learned a lot about pigeons from being around Richie.

"Richie?" I called out. He didn't respond. Was he asleep?

"Richie!" I said it louder this time. A few pigeons, disturbed by my voice, fluttered across the cage, and he turned around and looked...not really at me as much as through me. The sick pigeon was on his lap, in his hands. It wasn't moving. Had it died?

"I brought you breakfast," I said.

"Not hungry."

I put the tray down on the table. "Would it be all right if I joined you for a while?"

He didn't answer, so I took that as permission. I dragged a chair from the corner and set it down beside him. I was there to bring him breakfast, but there was one other reason I wanted to be there.

"Could I hold the pigeon?"

He hesitated for an instant and then handed me the bird. I held it carefully with both hands. It struggled a bit before settling in. It was good sign that it was struggling.

It was soft and warm. Shifting it to one hand, I used the other to gently stroke its feathers.

"Could I ask you a question?"

He didn't answer.

"Do you know about my mother and me leaving the estate?"

"July 1, 1950. It was Saturday."

"That's when we moved out?"

He nodded, looking at the bird in my hands.

"Do you know why my mother wanted to move?"

"She said she didn't want to be here," he said. "I wanted her to be here. She should have stayed here."

"But why did she leave? Why did we leave?"

"I told her not to go."

"But why did she want to go? Do you know why?"

"Because of him," he said.

"Him?"

"The man who killed her."

"My father? What did he have to do with it?"

"He came around and he wasn't supposed to."

"My father was here?"

"Around the guest house. He was trespassing, and my mother called the police. They took him. Twice."

I tried to figure out how my father coming here would cause my mother to move. Was she trying to get away from him or moving someplace where he could come around?

Suddenly, the little bird in my hands started to shake all over. Richie noticed right away. He took the bird from my hand. It continued to convulse.

"What's wrong?" I asked.

"It's dying." He brought the bird up close to his face. "I love you, little angel."

He twisted the bird in his hands, there was a loud snap, and it stopped moving. He'd broken its neck!

I gasped, unable to believe what I'd seen. Without saying another word, I got to my feet and rushed away, leaving him and the dead bird behind.

Twenty-One

I LEANED OVER, turning slightly to try to catch a glimpse of myself in the mirror as I stood atop the chair.

"Stay still or I'm going to prick you with a pin!" Mrs. Meyers said.

I straightened, but I really did want to see what the dress looked like—what I looked like. Looking down, I loved the way the skirt flared out. The material was so soft, like nothing I'd ever had against my skin before.

"I think the young officer is going to be suitably impressed," Mrs. Meyers said.

"I don't know. He might be."

"You don't like the dress?" she asked.

"I love the dress! It's just that, well, he might not be that impressed with me."

"You are an attractive young woman with a winning smile and a generous and kind nature. If he isn't impressed, then he's not worth impressing!" she said forcefully.

"Let him know two things," Nigel said as he turned away from the counter where he'd been cutting vegetables. "First, if I was thirty years younger he'd have to be fighting me off, and, second, if he doesn't treat you with respect, he'll be dealing with me." He held up the large knife he'd been using. "I can slice and dice as only a cook can!"

"You may have a large knife, but that officer has a gun," Mrs. Meyers said.

"That could be a problem. You know what they say—never take a knife to a gunfight!" he said. "But seriously, somebody has to talk to him when he comes to pick you up, and perhaps it should be me or James. You know, put a little fear of God in him."

"Somebody is going to speak to him," Mrs. Meyers said, sounding stern and looking rather scary and serious.

"Well, you are more formidable than either of us, so that works fine," Nigel said.

"Actually, it's not me," she said. "It's Mrs. Remington."

"Really?" I asked.

"She's rather insistent. She told me she wants to make sure he understands that while you're under her roof, you are like her daughter and will be treated with respect and care."

"I'm sure that isn't necessary," I said.

"Probably not, but you are in no position to argue with her. Even the mayor and chief of police don't argue with her," Mrs. Meyers said. "Besides, she's doing it because she cares for you."

"We all do," Nigel said.

That felt nice, so nice.

"I was wondering," Mrs. Meyers said, "if you don't mind me being a bit nosy, could I ask you a question?"

"Of course you can."

"Are you going to visit your father this week?"

That was the last question I expected. I thought it was going to be something about David. This was worse.

"I hadn't really thought about it." That was a lie, and I knew from experience that lies showed on my face. "Well, I haven't thought about it *much*." Another lie but less telling.

"So are you?" she asked.

"Mrs. Remington doesn't think I should visit him again."

"I wasn't asking what Mrs. Remington thought," she said. "I was asking what *you* thought. Do you want to visit him again?"

I nodded my head ever so slightly.

"When you do, can you say hello to him from me?" Nigel said from across the room.

"You knew him?"

"Kingston's a small place. I knew him pretty well. He was a little rough around the edges, and Lord knows with his size and reputation I wouldn't have wanted to get on his bad side."

The way my mother had gotten on his bad side, I thought.

"I always liked him," Nigel continued.

"I did as well," Mrs. Meyers said.

"But it doesn't really matter what the hired help thinks of somebody," Nigel added.

"You mean Mrs. Remington?" I asked.

"Mrs. Remington certainly didn't approve, but Edward simply *hated* him," Nigel said.

"And I guess I can understand that," Mrs. Meyers said. "They've always treated us like family, and they simply didn't think he was good enough for your mother."

"Can't blame them," Nigel said. "I wouldn't want my daughter being with a jailbird."

"He was in jail before this?"

"Maybe I shouldn't have said anything," Nigel said. He sounded like he felt guilty.

"No," Mrs. Meyers said. "She deserves to know as much truth as we have. He was imprisoned from right before you were born until you were almost three years old."

"What did he do?"

"Some form of assault. A bar fight gone bad. He nearly killed the man—beat him with his fists," Mrs. Meyers said.

"He didn't tell me that," I said.

"You and your mother used to visit him there."

"Where?"

"The Kingston jail. The same place you just visited."

My head felt like it was spinning. That was why it had seemed so familiar to me, especially the children.

"Your father's release from jail happened six months before you and your mother left," Mrs. Meyers said.

"Is that why we had to leave?" I asked. "Because of him?"

Both fell silent. Nigel suddenly became intensely interested in the vegetables he was chopping, while Mrs. Meyers focused on the pin work.

"I really want to know. Please, could you tell me why?"

Mrs. Meyers stopped working and looked right up at me. "I knew there was something troubling her, but she never told me what it was. One day she just packed up and left. She was here in the morning and gone by dinner."

"And she didn't say why?"

"She babbled about having to get on with her life, but there was something else, something that she wouldn't tell me," Mrs. Meyers said.

"There was a tremendous argument upstairs when she told Mrs. Remington," Nigel said.

"She was pretty upset when she couldn't convince Vicki to stay," Mrs. Meyers said. "When a woman has spent her life getting what she wants, it's hard to accept it when she can't. Besides, it was only because she thought she knew what was best for you and your mother."

"But she wasn't nearly as troubled as Edward and Richie," Nigel added. "Richie was a wreck, beside himself for weeks. He'd go off walking and be gone for the better part of the day. The two of you were a big part of his daily life, and you know how badly he reacts when routines are broken."

I knew how much a sick pigeon could unsettle him, so I couldn't even begin to imagine what he was like when we left. My thoughts went back to him snapping the neck of that pigeon.

"My father told me he was innocent," I said. "That he didn't do it."

"He said that throughout the trial," Mrs. Meyers said.

"Do you believe him?" I asked. "Do you think he *is* innocent?"

"I'm not in a position to know anything."

"My mother used to say that the best indication of the future is the past," Nigel said.

"What does that mean?"

"If you want to know what somebody is going to do in the future, you look to their past. Your father had a history of violence," he said.

"So you think he did it?"

"Nigel's in no better position than the rest of us to answer that question. But there's one person who might have more information," Mrs. Meyers said.

"Should I talk to Mrs. Remington?"

"Oh Lord, no!" she exclaimed. "I was thinking of your father."

"But how can I believe anything he says?"

"Maybe you can't. You'll have to judge, and the only way to do that is to go and visit him again," she said.

I knew Mrs. Remington would find out about the visit, and she would not be pleased. Still, he was my father, and I did want answers that maybe only he could give me.

There was a stomping sound by the back door. Ralph always stomped his feet before entering. The door opened and he said, "You have a visitor."

"I do?" Mrs. Meyers asked.

"Not you. Lizzy. He came to the back gate. He said his name is David, and he's wearing a police uniform."

I quickly changed out of my new dress and back into my old clothing. I didn't want him to see me in my maid's uniform. As I walked toward the back gate, I was excited to see him but also worried. Was he going to tell me that he wasn't able to take me to the dance? Had something come up, or had he simply thought better of going with me? I knew I certainly hadn't made the best impression— falling, crying and fainting after visiting my father, who was in prison for murdering my mother. Who could blame him? At least he wanted to tell me face-to-face. That would be hard, but it showed consideration and good manners on his part.

I stopped at the gate, the street still hidden by the hedges, and took a deep breath before proceeding. Whatever he said, I would be all right. I opened the gate, which made a loud creak, and stepped through. Just off to the side was the police car; David was leaning against the hood. He smiled and waved. As I walked toward him, he pulled a bouquet of flowers from behind his back.

I gasped. "Are those for me?"

"I tried to give them to the gardener, but he seemed even more surprised than you do."

He handed them to me.

"They're lovely. Thank you so much." Nobody had ever given me flowers before. Ever.

"I need to talk to you," he said.

"I understand if something came up and we can't go to the dance."

"I wouldn't let anything get in the way of something that important," he said. "Are you having second thoughts?"

"No, of course not! But why did you bring me flowers?"

"Because I saw them and they were beautiful and they reminded me of you."

I felt myself blush.

"I came because I have information I want to share with you before the dance. Information about your father. Come and have a seat."

He opened the door to the car and I sat down, which was good because my legs were feeling like jelly. What was he going to tell me? I'd thought I wanted more information, but now I wondered if I really did. He climbed in behind the wheel. It would have been easier if he'd simply told me he couldn't go to the dance.

"So I did a little bit of digging into the records," he began. "First off, you know your father was in prison before."

"I know. He was in there for beating somebody up." I didn't tell him I had only found out moments before.

"He'd been in jail a couple of times before that."

"I didn't know that."

"Nothing long term. A couple of days for public drunkenness, a two-week sentence for an altercation with a police officer, a weekend in jail for trespassing. And then there was the whole episode when he was arrested for murder.

It took five officers to take him down. Two of them were badly beaten, and he sent one to the hospital."

"That's awful."

"What makes it more awful is that the police officer he hospitalized went on to become the chief of police. My boss."

Was that what my father had meant when he said there were people who weren't going to let him out of prison early?

"Of course, in the end your father got worse than he gave. When he showed up in court, he was a mess—broken nose, a couple of shiners and a big gash on his head from where he'd been smacked by a billy club. They beat him pretty badly once they got him in the cell."

"That was in the records?"

He shook his head. "I met with a retired detective who worked the case, and he told me all sorts of things. Things that aren't necessarily on the record." He paused. "Things like the fact that your father had an alibi."

"I don't know what that means."

"He was in a bar drinking with some buddies at the time your mother was killed."

"Then he couldn't have done it—unless his friends were lying."

"Maybe they were mistaken. People really aren't reliable witnesses when they've been drinking. But his alibi would have held up if the murder weapon hadn't been found in a hole under a loose floor board in the closet of the room he was renting."

"So there's no doubt—none—that he did it," I said. I felt my heart drop.

"That's one of the interesting parts. They'd searched his house before and come up empty, and then they got a call telling them exactly where to look."

"Who called?"

"It was an anonymous phone call. The detective who worked the case said he thought it was peculiar, but they were happy to get a break. He said the police were under a lot of pressure from some powerful people." He pointed at the estate. "Before you and your mother moved out, there were two calls complaining about your father trespassing on their property, and apparently there was an incident between him and Edward Remington. It involved a weapon of some sort."

"My father pulled a weapon on Edward?"

He shook his head. "Edward pulled a weapon on him. If it had been the other way around, your father would have been arrested. As it was, the whole thing was recorded, but a note was made that Edward was simply defending his property against a trespasser, and your father spent the weekend in jail."

I didn't blame Edward for defending himself against my father, who was so big and, from everything I'd heard, somebody to be afraid of. Edward must have been trying to protect my mother and me. If only he'd been there the night of the murder. If my father had the chief of police, the mayor and the richest woman in town against him, then he was right: he'd stay in jail. I figured I should be grateful for what they were doing, but somehow it still didn't feel right.

"There's one other thing," he said. "And I know this may be hard to hear, because it's a detail about the murder itself. Do you want me to go on?"

"Yes," I said before I'd even stopped to think. Maybe I didn't. Maybe I should have at least asked what kind of detail it was.

"Okay, well, the hammer they found in his room matched the injuries to her...to the head. And there was blood. The same type as your mother's, so the coroner's office was sure it was the murder weapon. Even your father's defense attorney didn't argue that fact.

"What was strange, though, even stranger than the anonymous phone call, was that there were no fingerprints on the murder weapon. None. The handle had been wiped clean."

"But that makes no sense. Why would he have taken the time to wipe off his prints and then leave the blood on the head of the hammer? Why would he even keep it in the first place? Why wouldn't he have thrown it away?" I asked.

"I was thinking that too. The rooming house was practically on the lake. If he'd tossed it in the drink, nobody would ever have found it," David said.

"That is confusing."

"Even more confusing is, why a hammer in the first place? Your father is a huge man, a real brawler who was in a number of fights that were on the record and probably more that weren't."

"So why would he need a hammer to kill…to do that, right?"

"Right. He'd practically beaten one man to death and put a police officer in the hospital using his fists. It took five officers with clubs to finally subdue him. And in none of his prior incidents did he ever use a weapon. Why that night? Why would he use a hammer?"

"He wouldn't," I said. "So you think he didn't do it?"

"I'm just saying that I'm suspicious. I'd love to talk to your father."

"You could come with me the next time I go," I suggested.

"I'm not sure if I could discover anything of value, but at least you'd have somebody there with you."

"I'd like that."

"Then it's a date. A rather strange date, but still a date, although I don't think your father is going to be any too happy to see me."

"He knows you?"

He laughed. "Of course not. It's just that he doesn't seem to have a really good history with the police, and it's not going to make him any happier to find out his daughter is dating one."

"Dating?"

"Yeah. Our first date was when I drove you to the bank. The second was driving you home. This is our third date, and, of course, we have the dance coming up. We're practically an old married couple."

I felt myself go red all over, and I looked down at the ground. Toni had always kidded me that I went as red as a McIntosh apple when I was embarrassed.

David took my chin in his hand, gently moving my head upward until we were looking directly into each other's eyes.

"I'm sorry if I embarrassed you. Sometimes I talk too much. Please accept my apology, and I'll see you Saturday."

For an instant I thought he was going to draw me near and we were going to kiss, but he released me and said, "We both better get back to work."

Twenty-Two

I REACHED OVER and turned on the light on the night table; it took a few seconds for my eyes to adjust to the light. There was no point in even trying to sleep. I needed to talk to somebody, but it wasn't like I could talk to Mrs. Meyers or James or Nigel. The somebody I needed to talk to wasn't here. There was only one thing I could do.

I climbed out of bed, shuffled over to my desk and took out pen and paper.

Dear Toni,

It's two in the morning and I can't sleep. I can't even imagine I'm ever going to sleep again because I'm so excited. I just came home from the most incredible night of my life.

I guess I should start at the beginning. I met somebody. It was sort of an accident, but I got to know a young man. His name is David—Officer David Gibson. He's a police constable, and we met in the strangest way imaginable. He's very, very nice, and kind and funny and very considerate. He brought me flowers one day. He did first aid on my knee when I scraped it. He really is so kind. Depending on how you count them, we went on our first—or our fourth—date tonight. Either way, the one tonight was the best I could ever imagine. It was like something out of a movie.

He picked me up in his own car. He held the door open and he said nice things about my dress. I wish you could see my dress! Mrs. Meyers made it, and it's so beautiful. David thought it was beautiful too. He said I was beautiful. Me? Can you believe it? Not cute or attractive but beautiful. I had new white shoes and a white purse to go along with my new dress.

We went to a dance. A dance! All of those times you and I danced together, taking turns pretending we were the man, finally paid off, although there were a couple of times I started to lead. Despite being so big, he didn't step on my feet even once, which is a lot better than we used to do. We were on the dance floor almost all night, and when we weren't we sat at a table with three other couples. They were older police officers with their wives, but they were still so nice to me. David was even nicer. He pulled out my chair, and brought me punch, and when I said how much I liked the brownies, he went and got me a second one. He was such a gentleman, all night. Well, at least until the very end. He kissed me.

At the end of the night he drove me home and we stood outside the back door of the house and sort of shuffled around. I was really nervous because I thought he might try to kiss me. Actually, I hoped he would. He seemed as nervous as me, which

I thought was strange because he's so funny and handsome and he is a police officer and he is older—he's going to be twenty-one in less than two months.

The kiss wasn't long—just a couple of seconds—and I made sure to keep my lips closed, but it was so nice. I probably shouldn't have, but I was afraid I hadn't done it very well and I explained to him that it was my first kiss. He started to laugh, and I thought it was because I'd done so badly, but he told me that he'd only kissed two other girls a couple of times. Then I did something I can hardly believe I did—I reached up and kissed him! The second time was even better!

I'm going to see him again in two days. He's coming with me to do something difficult—to see my father in jail. Okay, maybe I have to explain all about that, but I don't really want to write about that now. That's going to have to wait for another letter at another time because I can't even think about anything except tonight.

Right now I just wanted you to know one thing and only one thing. I got my first kiss! And I guess I gave my first kiss too.

I hesitated for a minute, thinking about how to sign the letter. Should it be Betty or—then I knew.

With much love,
Lizzy
P.S. I miss you so much. Please, please, please write back soon. I need to know that you are safe and your life is going well.

I'd done it. Not only finished the letter but signed my name—my real name. Lizzy. That was who I was. I put down the pen, folded the letter and placed it into an envelope. Tomorrow I'd address it, put on a stamp and mail it. I laid it down on the desk. I just wished I could be there to see Toni's reaction when she opened it. I hoped she was doing as well as I was. I was sure she was. After all, she was the strong one. I so wanted to know what was going on in her life.

I went back to my bed, climbed in, pulled up the covers and turned off the light. I didn't know if sleep would come any easier now, but I'd have to try. Morning was going to come quickly, and I'd promised to help with breakfast even though it was my day off.

Twenty-Three

"ARE YOU EVER going to stop smiling?" Mrs. Meyers asked.

"I've been told I always smile."

"Not as much as you have this morning. Obviously, things went well last night at the dance."

"Yes, they did. It was very nice."

"I thought as much when you came in so late."

"I'm so sorry if I woke you!"

"No waking involved. It didn't feel right going to sleep until I knew you were safe and sound at home."

"You didn't need to do that!"

"I didn't need to, but I wanted to," she said.

"I didn't mean to put you to any trouble."

"It's not trouble. It's a pleasure to have somebody to worry about and fuss over—at least, somebody who isn't an old woman who's my boss."

She placed a flower in a little crystal vase on the tray, along with Mrs. Remington's breakfast, which was covered to keep the meal warm. Mrs. Remington had sent down word through Richie that she wanted breakfast in bed this morning.

"There, all done," she said. "You take it up to her."

"Me?" Mrs. Meyers always took her Sunday breakfast up to her.

"That's too many steps for me this early in the morning."

I knew there was more to it than that, but I didn't think it would be respectful to ask. I picked up the tray and started up the back stairs leading to the second floor.

The stairs were very narrow and steep. They certainly weren't like the main staircases in the mansion. These steps were built so that servants could do their jobs without being seen or heard, but they weren't built for comfort. At the top of the stairs I came out into the hall right beside the door to the master bedroom. It was closed, and I knocked.

"Come," she called from within.

Balancing the tray with one hand, I opened the door and entered. "Good morning, ma'am. It's Lizzy."

"I know," she said. "I asked that you bring me my breakfast this morning. You'll have to forgive me for being a nosy old woman, but I wanted to ask you about last night, if you don't mind."

"Of course I don't mind," I said, "although I do object to you calling yourself nosy. It's very kind of you to be interested in me, and I appreciate it."

I gently placed the tray on her lap and fluffed up the pillows, placing them behind her.

"You, Lizzy, are as kind as your mother, and I am very interested in your well-being. Did you have a good time?"

"Wonderful. We danced and danced and danced."

"My late husband and I loved to dance. And was your escort a gentleman?"

"A perfect gentleman."

"If he hadn't been, I would have had a few words with his chief. I may be old-fashioned, but I feel that I have an obligation to keep you safe. I just wish that I could have kept..."

"My mother safe?"

She nodded.

"I know that if you had had your way, she would have stayed on at the guest house and she would still be alive," I said.

"That is one of the biggest regrets of my life. I should have been more persuasive, more convincing, but I wasn't." She inhaled and exhaled deeply. "The past is the past. We can only deal with the present and the future. Have you given any more thought to your future, to going on for further education?"

"I was talking to David—Officer Gibson last night about nursing. He said that the police have dealings with nurses at the hospital and he and the other officers have such high respect for them."

"There is nobility in the profession. I think you'd be a fine nurse. We must keep focused on the future and not allow the past to cause unnecessary detours or trouble."

I knew she was talking about my father and the visits. I didn't want to disappoint her after all the kindness she'd shown me. Yet even if I didn't tell her, she'd know within a day of the visit. I had to tell her, but I had to explain it properly.

I took a deep breath. "I'm going to visit my father tomorrow. I'm not going to go very often, maybe never again, but I have to go at least once more."

"I understand the desire, but not the purpose."

"He told me he was innocent, that he didn't do it."

She laughed. "That man is far from innocent. Don't you think a murderer could also be a liar?"

"I guess he could be."

"Guess?" she snapped. "Of course he's lying, because…" She let the sentence trail away and started again. This time her voice was calm and gentle. "I understand that you want to believe him, it's only natural, but if you knew about his history of violence and the previous times he'd spent in jail, then you'd—"

"I do know," I said, cutting her off.

She gave me a questioning look. Had I revealed something I shouldn't have? Now there was no choice but to tell her how I knew.

"David told me about the three years my father served in prison for nearly killing somebody, and the other offenses, about him coming around here and Edward making him leave."

"Edward stepped forward to put himself between danger and you and your mother. Did your father tell you that he threatened Richie?"

"Why would he threaten Richie?"

"That's a question you might want to ask him if you do decide to follow through with that visit. You need to use your head and not your heart. If your mother had only listened to our warnings then, well, none of this would have happened."

"David is coming with me," I blurted out.

"And why would he do that?"

I almost told her about his suspicions, about the unexplained details of the case, but I didn't.

"David said the same thing you did about my father claiming he was innocent. He said that everybody in prison says they're innocent. He wants to be there for me," I said.

"He is a considerate young man. It will be helpful for you to have outside ears to hear, outside eyes to see and a policeman's mind to think. You might want to listen to that young man. Obviously, he is concerned enough and caring enough to want to be there. He must be worried about you. I'm worried about you, Lizzy. I couldn't live with myself if I allowed your father to harm you in any way. I only have your best interests at heart."

"I know that, and I'm very grateful for your caring and kindness. I'm sorry that I've caused you so much distress," I said.

"No need to apologize for that," she said. "Perhaps you should apologize for causing my breakfast to get cold though." She lifted the tray. "I'd like you to have all of this warmed up."

Twenty-Four

I CAME OUT of the bank and looked around for David.
He was nowhere to be seen. He'd warned me he might be a
little late, so there was nothing to do but wait. In my purse
was my bank book. I had deposited all of my pay—$35—plus
an additional $15 I had held back before, so my account was
now an even $300. It felt good to have that much money.
It was comfort, defense, a shield against anything that
could go wrong, but also something that could help make
things go right.

I'd spent a great deal of time thinking about the offer
Mrs. Remington had made to help me become a nurse.
Staying at the house and working part-time would provide
me with room and board and a small stipend for pocket
money. Kingston General Hospital was within walking
distance of the house, so I wouldn't need money for trans-
portation. I simply needed to pay for my tuition, books and
uniform. Mrs. Meyers had helped me find out all the costs.

Mrs. Remington had offered to loan me money, but I wanted to do it myself. I'd calculated—with Mrs. Meyers's help—that if I saved $950, that would be enough.

Mrs. Remington had also told me that she'd spoken to the president of the hospital, the head of admissions and the dean of the nursing program. They had all assured her that if I applied I would be admitted. All that remained was raising some money and getting confirmation that I had been granted my high-school diploma. I'd know soon enough, and if I didn't get my diploma—well, it was possible to get it through correspondence courses, even though it would take at least a year. If the fire had happened only a month later, I would have graduated and had my diploma in hand.

Of course, it wouldn't be the worst thing to just stay here and work for another year. Everybody was so kind, so nice to me, and it seemed like every day I learned more about my mother or me, and I was saving money. And on top of that there was David.

Still, it would be hard if I had to go that route. A car tapped its horn, and I looked up to see David pulling into the parking lot. I ran over to the car, and before I could get there he'd gotten out and opened up the door for me.

"You look very nice today," he said.

"Thank you." I was wearing another "new" dress, something else that Mrs. Meyers had crafted. It was more formal and proper, the sort of dress one would wear for going to the bank, but it was also very lovely. David was dressed in a suit jacket and tie. He looked like he was going to church.

As we drove, we talked.

"I'm a little nervous about all of this," David said.

"I guess it is a little strange going to visit somebody in jail."

"It's not just that. I'm meeting my girlfriend's father."

I laughed. "Your girlfriend?"

"Technically, you are my *friend* and there's no denying you are a *girl*, and we did go to the dance on Saturday, and this is, by my count, our fifth date in the past week…so what do you think that makes you?"

"I guess your girlfriend," I said. "Which would make you my boyfriend." Oh, my goodness, I had a boyfriend!

The walls of the prison loomed up on the left side of the road and all the talk of boyfriend and girlfriend ended with the seriousness of what we were about to do. David pulled the car up into a parking lot across the street from the entrance.

"Here we are," he said. "It's not too late to change your mind if you don't want to go inside."

"It's not so much *want* to as *need* to. But you don't have to go in if you don't want to."

"I need some answers too."

We made our way to the first counter. I'd made sure this time that we were there a full thirty minutes before visitation was to begin. David said he wanted to have a few words with the guards as we entered. The same guard as before, looking as sour as before, was behind the counter. But when he saw us, to my shock he smiled. Instinctively I smiled back.

"Good to see you're here early. Gord will be happy to have you back. And who are you?" he asked, pointing a finger at David.

"I'm here to meet my girlfriend's father."

"And to keep me company," I added.

David pulled out his wallet and flashed the guard his badge.

"I don't recognize you," the guard said, "and I thought I knew everybody on the force."

"I'm new. I'm here to support Lizzy, but I was also hoping to ask the prisoner a few questions."

That word—*prisoner*—seemed harsh, but that was what he was. My father was a prisoner.

"Not that common for a police officer to ask questions of somebody who was convicted a dozen years ago. What's this investigation about?" he asked.

"It's not so much an investigation as just some questions that Lizzy needs answered," David said.

"This can't be easy. Tell you what. I'm going to show you a little professional courtesy here—you know, prison guard to cop," the guard said. "I'm going to arrange for a private room for the interview."

"That's kind of you," David said.

"Just respect my badge if I get pulled over for speeding some time," the guard said.

"As far as I'm concerned, you and your buddies can drag race down Princess Street and I'll look the other way."

"I might just hold you to it. You know, Gord is a pretty straight shooter. No problems, no hassles, no headaches. He's doing hard time but not giving anybody a hard time."

"I really appreciate that," David said. "We both do."

"Yes, thank you so much," I said.

"There will be a guard present, and you will be expected not to make any contact. The same rules apply," the guard said.

"We understand," I said. "And thank you."

⁓

We sat and waited. The room wasn't very big, with four chairs, two on each side of a large wooden table, concrete walls painted green, the paint peeling off in places, and a high ceiling soaring above us. The place felt cold and damp, which might have explained the peeling paint and the goose bumps on my arms.

David reached over and took my hand, intertwining my fingers with his. The room was suddenly warmer. I was about to speak when the door opened—it was my father, followed by a guard. My father smiled at me and then looked at David before setting his gaze on me again.

"I'm so glad to see you, Lizzy," he said. "Who is this?"

David got up and reached out his hand. "I'm David—"

"No contact!" the guard snapped.

David drew back his hand. "Sorry, I wasn't thinking." He sat back down.

"David is my friend," I said.

"Hello, sir," David said.

"Are you my daughter's boyfriend?"

"Yes, sir."

"I'm not sure how I feel about my daughter dating a cop."

The guards must have told him about David.

"How did you know I'm a police officer?" David asked.

"I can pick out a cop from across the room," my father said. "You all look pretty much the same."

"I guess you could say the same thing about prisoners," David said. "Doesn't mean that some of them can't be different."

"I don't have the time or energy to find out. Why don't you wait outside so me and my daughter can visit?"

"I want him here," I said. "Besides, David has some questions for you."

"I thought the father was supposed to be asking the questions," he said. "Why should I talk to you at all?"

"Because I asked him to be here, because maybe he can help," I said.

"I've never had a cop help me, so I'm not sure why that would happen now."

"Maybe he can help you, but I need his help too. Please, could you answer his questions?"

He didn't respond right away, and I was worried about what he was going to say—or do. Was he going to walk away? Was my second visit going to be my last?

"I guess it depends on what sort of questions," he said.

"I have some questions about the crime and the conviction," David said.

"There's not much point in talking about any of that. It's not like it's going to change anything."

"Lizzy told me you said you were innocent," David said.

"I *am* innocent."

"I was going through the case records—"

"They're reopening the investigation?" he asked.

"No, I was going through them myself," David said.

My father laughed. "Is that so you could impress my daughter, to show her what a big important man you are?"

"It isn't that—" I started to say.

"That was part of it in the beginning," David said, surprising me. "But that's not why I'm here. Your alibi was some friends at a bar. Were any of them called as witnesses at the trial?"

"Four of them. They all confirmed I was there with them in the hours around the time of the murder."

"Four witnesses certainly sounds like a pretty good defense," David said.

"I had practically no defense. My lawyer was useless. He just sat there while the four of them were made out to be a bunch of rounders, too drunk to remember and willing to lie to protect me."

"And were they?" David asked.

"They were in a bar, so of course they were drinking, and maybe they weren't the best people in the city," my father said, "but they were telling the truth, and my lawyer allowed the Crown to convince the jury differently. I wonder if he was paid to throw the case."

"Do you still have contact with any of the witnesses?" David asked.

"Regular contact with one of them. He's inside, one cell block over. If he wasn't believable before he certainly isn't now."

"And the others?"

"I have no idea what happened to them or where they are, although I suspect they didn't go too far," he said. "They were all born and raised in Kingston and probably didn't go much farther away than I did."

"What if I go through the case files, try to find their last addresses as well as their names and try to re-interview them? See what they remember."

"None of that will do any good. The court didn't believe them then and it's not going to believe them now."

"But I might," David said. "Besides, what have you got to lose?"

"Not much. But why are you doing any of this?" my father asked.

"I'm just looking for the truth for Lizzy's sake," David said. "Some things don't make sense."

"Like what?" my father asked.

"Like why would you wipe the fingerprints off the handle of the hammer but not the blood? Why didn't you throw it away?" I asked.

"That's the sort of question I thought other people should have asked," he said. "You're starting to believe me, aren't you?"

"All I believe is that I need answers," I said. I could tell by his expression that I'd surprised him with my boldness. I'd surprised myself.

"Then I'll give them to you. I never saw that hammer until it showed up as an exhibit in court. Somebody put that hammer there, planted evidence, set me up," he said.

"It all sounds suspicious, but who would want to set you up?" David asked.

"Obviously, the same person who did the killing. Who else would have had the hammer? He wanted the crime put on my head to protect himself."

"But who would want to kill her?" David asked.

"I've spent over thirteen years thinking about that, and I haven't been able to come up with an answer that makes sense. Nobody wanted her dead." He turned to me. "Your mother was the kindest person I knew. She had no enemies. Everybody loved her; she trusted everybody, maybe too much."

"What does that mean?" David asked, saying exactly what I was thinking.

"Do you know why I'm here?" my father asked.

"You were convicted of murder," David said.

"Funny. Half the people in the clink are here either because they didn't have the money and connections to get off or they got in the way of people with money and connections. Your mother trusted some people she shouldn't have."

That was exactly what Mrs. Remington had said about my mother trusting my father.

"Are you talking about specific people or just some sort of conspiracy of the rich against the poor?" David asked.

"Very specific and very rich. They control the city. The people she worked for," he said.

"The Remingtons?" I asked.

"Yeah, you've obviously heard of them."

"I live at their mansion. I'm a maid there, like my mother was."

His expression changed to complete shock, then fear. "No...no, you can't be there. You have to get away from them!" His voice got louder with each word. The guard who was sitting in the corner rose to his feet. "All she wanted was to get away from there."

"Why did she leave, why did we move away?" I asked.

"She was desperate to get out of that house."

"But why?"

He shook his head. "She wouldn't tell me. I think she didn't want to tell me because of how I might react, but I know she was afraid."

"Afraid of what?" David asked.

"I don't know, but I have an idea. That son, that strange one—I think it was him."

"But everybody told me that Richie was more upset than anybody about her leaving," I said.

"She wouldn't tell me, but I think it was the way he was acting that made her want to leave. I don't know what kind of different he is, but he's definitely different," my father said.

"Do you think he was the one who committed the crime?" David asked.

"I considered that," my father said. "But really, isn't he too slow to pull off something like that?"

David turned to me. "You know him better than we do. What do you think?"

I felt my whole body stiffen. I wondered if David would mention Richie hitting the squad car with a shovel. Should I tell them about his breaking the pigeon's neck, or how difficult he got when routines were broken—routines like my mother and me living there?

"I don't know. I know he's different, but I don't know. I could try to figure it out, spend more time with him and—"

"No!" my father exclaimed, cutting me off. "You need to leave there. I'll do my time. It doesn't matter. You need to be safe!" He jabbed a finger at David and suddenly jumped to his feet. "You need to get her out of there, find her a place to go, another job, anything! Just get her away from that house!" he yelled.

The guard rushed over to his side. He was holding the billy club in his hand.

"That's it! This visit is over!" he ordered.

There was a look on my father's face that I couldn't even describe—rage, worry, upset, anguish all rolled into one frightening expression. His whole body seemed to get larger; his shoulders went back, and his fingers curled into fists.

Was he going to strike out or—? He let out a big sigh and, like air escaping from a balloon, his whole body sagged and his fingers uncurled.

"Sure, boss, no problem," he said to the guard. With that, the guard seemed to relax as well.

My father sat back down. "I want to thank you both for coming. It means so much to me to have you here again. I love you, little angel."

I felt my whole body melt.

He turned directly to David. "You're going to have to keep her safe. It's your job. If anything happens to her, these walls and that badge aren't going to be enough to keep you alive."

There was hardness in his eyes, and I saw David shrink back into his seat. I wasn't the only one who believed what my father had just said. He got to his feet again—this time slowly. He walked over to the guard and they left the room.

David took my hand. "I'm not going to let anybody harm you."

Twenty-Five

AS DAVID STARTED to drive away after taking me back to the mansion, I waved him down, and he skidded to a stop. I ran over and leaned in his window.

"I just wanted to thank you for everything, for being there, for caring, for understanding, for driving me all around this afternoon."

We'd driven for two hours after the visit with my father. I didn't want to return to the house before I'd calmed down.

"It's no big deal. Just trying to help my girlfriend." He gave me a big, bright smile.

I gave him one more kiss.

"If you want, you can climb back in and we can go for a longer drive," he said.

"I wish I could. I have to go in and help with dinner. I've been gone too long already."

"We'll talk. Soon. You'll be fine—there's nothing to worry about."

"I know. I know."

He reached out and gave my arm a squeeze. Releasing it, he put the car in gear, and I stepped aside. I watched him drive away. I felt alone and afraid. I turned and faced the rear gate, framed by the high hedges. Behind it was the house. The one my father wanted me to leave. The one my mother had left, taking me with her. I didn't have to go through that gate. I didn't need to go into that house. Was there really something for me to fear?

I'd only gone a few steps when I caught sight of Ralph working on one of the flower beds. He looked up and waved, and I waved back. There was nothing for me to worry about. Inside the house were Mrs. Meyers, James, Nigel and Ralph, Mrs. Remington and Richie. These people—all of them—cared for me.

I stopped once again at the door and gave my face another rub. I was pretty sure I'd gotten rid of the signs of tears. Thank goodness I hadn't cried the night of the dance, or David would have thought I cried every time I saw him.

He had been so good today, so supportive, so understanding, so kind. He'd said reassuring things but tried to keep me level-headed. He was going to try to track down those witnesses and talk to them further. Maybe they had lied at the trial for my father and now, with years past and him in jail, there was no point in lying anymore. He was going to take that old detective out for another coffee and ask him more questions. He promised me he'd get answers, even if the answers might not be what I wanted them to be.

I wanted my father to be innocent, to have been arrested unjustly. It would make me feel better, would help me understand why I was abandoned. Still, what I really wanted was to know the truth about my father.

My *father*. I turned the word around in my mind. It was as foreign as the word *mother*. I didn't remember my mother, but she seemed more real to me than the man I'd met twice. Everybody told me how much I looked like her, acted like her, even laughed and sounded like her. But him? That hulking man sitting across the table from me, that man who had been jailed before for violence, who had been convicted of murdering my mother, well, was he really even my father?

I took one more deep breath and then opened the door and entered. "Sorry I'm a little late!"

Mrs. Meyers was at the counter and Nigel at the stove. Both turned and gave me welcoming smiles.

"Not a problem," Nigel said. "We managed without you for over a decade, so a few minutes isn't going to matter."

"There's something there on the table for you," Mrs. Meyers said.

There was a big brown envelope. Even from this distance I recognized the writing on the front. Big, flowing, graceful— Mrs. Hazelton!

I rushed over and grabbed the envelope. It was bigger than a regular letter. In fact, it was the same size as the envelope she'd given me before, back in her study on that fateful day. I found myself struck by a terrible fear. Was it going to contain more information about my past? I shook my head slightly at my own silly thoughts. That couldn't be it. I knew that.

I'd always admired Mrs. Hazelton's graceful script. It was still beautiful, but I could see a slight wavering in the letters and could picture the shaking of her hand. She was getting weaker, sicker. Would I ever see her again?

"Unless you're like Superman and you have X-ray vision, you're going to have to open that envelope to know what's inside," Nigel said.

I turned it over and carefully tore it open at the top. There was a large sheet of thick paper inside. I pulled it out. At first it didn't make sense.

Then I gasped. "Oh my goodness!"

"What is it?" Mrs. Meyers asked.

"It's a diploma, a secondary-school graduation diploma." I turned it around so she could see it, and she took it from me.

"Not just a diploma but an honors diploma. You must have been a very good student. It says, *This honors graduation diploma is granted to Elizabeth Anne Roberts.*"

"Elizabeth Anne. But how did the school know to put on my real name?"

"Probably that matron of yours," Mrs. Meyers said.

"Mrs. Hazelton."

"Yes, she must have arranged it."

"Never look a gift horse in the mouth," Nigel added.

"But there must be more." I turned the envelope over, and a folded page fell out. I unfolded it. It *was* from Mrs. Hazelton.

Dear Betty...or should I say Elizabeth,

Congratulations on obtaining your diploma. I was so very pleased when I saw that you received honors. As I always said, hard work will lead to rewards.

You must be pleased to receive your diploma. All of the girls successfully completed their school year and either received a diploma or the credits for course work completed. I thought it was unfair that circumstances beyond your control could have stopped all of you from reaching goals that were not only important but imminent and deserved. I spoke first to the principal, who was less than agreeable to my suggestion. There was a subsequent conversation with the superintendent of education and finally the director of education.

My discussion basically centered upon what would happen if a student a few weeks from graduation fell too ill to take the exams. They said that all previous marks would be summed and if sufficient, regardless of marks to be gained through the examinations, a graduation diploma would be issued. In review, all of you girls had sufficient marks to pass without having to complete the final examinations, so really they had no choice but to relent.

There was a further complication with your diploma, as I wished it to be awarded in your real name. I know you have plans beyond secondary school, and I wanted this diploma to be your "invitation" to go further. I expect you to go further.

I will not bother you with an account of how I am faring, but it is suffice to say that I continue to move forward. As I know you will.

I look forward to finding out more about how life is proceeding for you, and be assured that I will reply and that you remain in my thoughts every day.

With affection,

Agnes Hazelton

"Congratulations!" Mrs. Meyers said. "Does this mean you could go to nursing school this fall?"

"I don't think I'll have enough savings."

"As I recall, Mrs. Remington said she would provide you sufficient support regardless of your savings. Correct?"

I thought back to our conversation, but all the details seemed vague—she had offered that, hadn't she? Everything seemed foggy. Things kept rushing at me, overwhelming me. Just when I tried to make sense of one thing, something else came up.

"Are you going to open the other letter?" Mrs. Meyers asked.

"Other letter?" I turned around to the table. There was another envelope—this one white and smaller—sitting beside where the first had been. It had been blocked by the larger envelope and I hadn't seen it. The writing on it was as distinctive as Mrs. Hazelton's. It was from Toni!

Twenty-Six

I EXCUSED MYSELF, left the others in the kitchen and retreated to my bedroom. I hoped they didn't think I was rude, but I needed to be someplace private to read Toni's letter. Closing the door behind me, I was alone. Just me and Toni's letter. It felt right. It was like the two of us together in the room, sharing secrets once again.

Carefully, so as not to rip it, I opened the envelope and slipped out the letter. I wanted to read it, to hear how wonderfully she was doing, but I was afraid—what if things were going badly? How could I help her? Well, there was only one way to know if she needed help. I unfolded the letter.

Dear Betty,

Things are so unbelievable here in Toronto that I don't know where to begin! It's all good, mainly.

I let out a sigh of relief. That was what I needed to know, that things were good. I turned back to the letter.

Well, actually, it's a bit of a roller coaster, and I'm still having the nightmares. But still good, you know? All in all, I'm pretty proud of myself. Like, there's a billion people in this city and I even know some of them! I have this amazing huge room, but I'm the only one in it, which is good except when I'm lonely and when I have the dreams.

Anyway, when the dreams are really bad (you know, me screaming my head off), a very nice man who is a professor of literature at the University of Toronto comes down and knocks on my door until I wake up and answer it. Isn't that sweet? I live in sort of a rooming house, but it's just me and the professor who board here. Mrs. Grady Vespucci owns 75 Hazelton and she is the most beautiful woman you could possibly imagine, except she drinks a bit too much. She calls them "refreshments" but they're spirits, Betty, no two ways about it. Grady gives me fashion advice and life advice and I tell her most everything when she hasn't over-refreshed.

She wrote about the people she worked with and some musicians and a guy named Cassidy—that was the important part for her. She also mentioned someone named Ethan, the son of a Mr. Brooks Goldman, who was...

...this amazing musician whose band, The Ramblers, plays at the Purple Onion all the time and who, embarrassingly,

I thought was my father for a minute. I also thought that Ian Tyson was my father (same amount of time). Don't ask—it was HUMILIATING! I know, I know...I'm the one that teased you all for your stupid orphan fantasies, but get me out of the orphanage and my imagination goes haywire! Maybe it's the alone thing. So in the end, unlike you, I haven't made much progress in finding out who my real father is or was, and I haven't tried real hard on the mother front. Actually, I am trying to track a lady down who was her best friend, but it's complicated—she's in a ladies' prison!

I am so glad to hear that you are well settled with people who care about you. I am even gladder to hear that you have a young man! David sounds wonderful and the FIRST KISS sounds spectacular (I'm more than a little jealous)!!! I have a young man, too, except he's older. Cassidy (it has just hit me that I don't know what his last name is!) is a businessman, and he might be almost thirty! I know, I know...But he is SUCH a gentleman, and everybody looks when I'm with him because he is so handsome, and I'm not exaggerating for once. He is going to take me to a very posh party one day, and I'm already fretting about what to wear. He hasn't kissed me yet—as I say, he is a true gentleman. He is very, very interested in my story about being an orphan. He really cares. I believe he will try to help me.

Anyway, anyway, I miss you to pieces and more. Actually, I miss all of us as an "us" more than I ever thought possible. I dreamed of being away and on my own, of having my own room, for such a long time and now that I finally have it...well, it's just not like I thought it would be is all. Tell your fella I said hi and to treat you like a queen. Good luck at your end with everything, and write me soon if not sooner.

Love you lots,

Toni

xoxox ·

I put the letter down. It wasn't long, but what I'd really needed to hear was in the first line. I'd show it to David and tell him hello from Toni. I felt better—and maybe a little uneasy.

Who was this Cassidy fellow, and were his intentions really honorable? He was awfully old. I wished I could meet him and judge for myself. Wait, that wasn't just some silly fantasy. I could meet him. I could take the train to Toronto— or, better yet, have David drive me—and he could meet Toni. That really wasn't so far-fetched. I knew it couldn't happen quite yet, but I'd write to Toni about that very thing in my next letter to her. Maybe I hadn't had a chance to say goodbye, but I'd soon have a chance to say hello.

Twenty-Seven

I SETTLED INTO bed, thinking about writing to Toni to tell her all that had happened since my last letter and to ask her for advice. At dinner Mrs. Remington had made it clear that I had her full financial support if I decided to go to school in the fall. I hadn't want to take her offer, but now I wasn't so sure. She kept peppering me with questions about going to school this fall.

There was a tap on the door, and before I could respond, the door slowly opened and Mrs. Meyers peeked in.

"I saw the light under the door, so I thought you'd still be awake," she said.

"With all that's happened, I don't know if I'll be able to sleep for the next week."

She laughed. "It has been quite the rush of events in your time here."

And that only included the parts she knew about. I'd told her bits about the visit at the prison. There were actually a couple of things I wanted to ask her, and I'd have to reveal a bit more to get any information.

"My father said that my mother left here because she was afraid," I said.

Mrs. Meyers didn't answer. She didn't even look at me.

"Was she?" I asked.

She nodded her head slightly. "She was pretty spooked at the end."

"By what?"

"Some people thought it was your father."

"That doesn't make sense."

"Don't be blind to who he is," she said. "He's a very imposing, threatening man."

"I know his history, but if she was afraid of him, why would she leave here, where she was safe, to go out there, where she'd be less safe?"

"I don't have an answer to that."

"You run from danger to where you think you're safe, not the other way around," I said. "Whatever she was afraid of must have been here."

I paused. What I was going to say couldn't be unspoken. I needed to say it the right way.

"Was she afraid of Richie?" I asked.

Mrs. Meyers didn't answer, but she did look more uncomfortable. She got up and walked to the door. I thought she was leaving, but she closed the door and came back and sat down on the edge of the bed right beside me.

"I'm going to say this quietly," she said, her voice barely a whisper. "Sometimes I think these walls have ears." She leaned in even closer. "There have been times in the past when Richie has been more *difficult*."

"More difficult than hitting a police car with a shovel?"

"Much more, but it was years and years ago," she said.

"All of this happened years and years ago. Was my mother afraid of Richie?"

"You have to understand, he's not a mean boy, but sometimes he just doesn't understand things—he doesn't understand people or emotions. He would never intentionally hurt anybody, but he's just so big and—"

"Did he hurt my mother?"

"Never. He loved your mother. Probably more than he loved anything except those fool pigeons of his. It's just that sometimes he crowded her too much, wanted her around too much."

"And that's why she left?"

"I can't be certain, but I think it could have been that. At the end, she always wanted me to be around. That last week before she left and took you away, I agreed to sleep out in the guest cottage."

"Then she was afraid."

"She was, but I thought then that she was afraid of your father coming in the middle of the night."

"And now?"

She shook her head. "I don't know. It's all so confusing. After the two of you left, it got even worse around here.

Edward was beside himself with worry, and Richie just kept leaving. Sometimes he'd be gone well into the middle of the night."

The middle of the night—the time when my mother was—

"He couldn't have done it," she said, answering my unasked question. "He would never have harmed your mother, no matter what."

"What if he didn't mean to? What if he just struck out without thinking, the way he did at the police car?"

She didn't answer right away, but I could tell she was thinking. "What you are suggesting is possible. But you have to understand the reason I'm sure Richie couldn't have done this. I know the details of the case. I wish I didn't know them. Even if Richie did commit the crime—which I don't think he did—is there any way on God's green earth that he could have covered it up? I remember from the testimony that your father claimed the hammer was planted in his room. There is no way Richie is capable of doing that."

There *was* no way. Not in a million years.

"Let's just keep this conversation to ourselves, all right?" she asked. "There is no need to bring this up with Nigel or James, and you certainly don't want to talk to Mrs. Remington about this at all!"

"I'd never dream of doing that!"

"Good, because she wants to see you."

"What does she want to talk about?" Suddenly I felt guilty.

"My guess is about your schooling. She is nothing less than a dog with a bone when she gets something on her mind."

"What do you think I should do?"

"I think you'd be a fool not to accept her offer. Besides, in the end, Mrs. Remington always gets what she wants, so why fight it?"

~

I tapped gently on the door, almost hoping that she'd already gone to sleep.

"Come," she said.

I entered. "You wanted to see me, ma'am?"

"Yes. Come here; sit down right beside me." She patted the bed.

I eased myself onto the bed.

"You need to know two things about me, possibly things you already know. One, I almost always get what I want."

Almost exactly what Mrs. Meyers had said.

"Two, I care deeply for you. You've only been here for a short time now, but you were here for years before. You are like a daughter or a granddaughter, one who has been returned to me."

I felt my whole body melt. She reached out and took both of my hands in hers.

"And because of that, I must do for you what I would do for a daughter. What I would have done for your mother, if only I'd had the chance. It's so sad that I had planned to go over, the day after it happened, to make her the same offer I've made to you, to help her return to school, and also to ask her to move back to our property."

I held my breath.

"Starting in September you *will* go to nursing school. I am going to pay for tuition, books and a uniform and provide you with a living allowance."

"I can't allow you—"

"Weren't you listening to the two things I just said to you? You *are* going to go to school, and I *am* going to pay. These are not subjects for debate. Understood?"

"I don't know what to say."

"That is simple. You will say yes and thank you very much."

I laughed. "Yes, and thank you very much."

"I'm so glad you're not going to argue. It's agreed then. You're going to nursing school in the fall. I have your word, correct?"

"Yes. I don't know how I'll ever be able to repay you."

"You'll be repaying me by going on to live a wonderful life. Perhaps in my older age you might even become my nurse," she said.

"I'd do that!"

"That was simply a joke. I'm doing for you what I'd do for any of my children. That's what you have to understand, and perhaps you won't fully until you have children of your own, but a mother will do anything for her children. *Anything.*" She emphasized that last word clearly.

"Which leads me to the last thing we need to talk about. The final, obvious topic."

I looked around anxiously, not knowing what she meant.

"Don't worry, dear. I want to talk to you about your visit today."

Of course she knew I'd been at the jail today, but how much did she know?

"Sometimes when a man is drowning, the first thing the rescuer does is knock him unconscious with a punch to the face," she said.

"Why would they do that?" I questioned. And why would Mrs. Remington be talking about this?

"Because the person who is drowning will flail around in such panic that they can ensnare the rescuer, harm them, even knock them unconscious, and so, in that desperate attempt to not drown, they both die. Do you understand what I'm saying?"

Suddenly, I did. "You think my father will harm me."

"You and anybody else he can reach. He's grasping at straws, trying to lay blame anywhere but on himself. Can you imagine anybody believing it was Richie who harmed your mother?"

I was shocked, and I let out a little gasp. How did she know?

"Prison walls are thick, but not so thick that I don't hear things. The guard is the son of people my husband helped many years ago, and he felt an obligation to let me know what was said. As I told you before, this really is more like a small town than a city, and we have helped so many people, the way I'm going to help you. You don't believe what your father said about my son, do you?"

I shook my head. I didn't now.

"Richie would never have harmed your mother. He— both my boys—*adored* her. Besides, Richie couldn't have done it. He was with me. We were in Montreal that night."

"I didn't know that."

"How could you, dear?" she asked. "It's all in the police report. I took him away because I thought a change of scenery would make him feel better. Of course it didn't. I just wish I could have been there for your mother." A tear leaked out of the corner of her eye.

"Believe me, if I could take back one thing that happened in my life, it is the death of your mother. There is hardly a day that goes by when I don't think about her. What I'm offering is for you and for your mother. Your mother would be *so* proud of you. The way I'm proud of you."

Would my father be proud of me? Should I even care?

"Remember, your future lies in front of you. Behind are only shadows, fears and regrets. We have so much to do, and I'd like you to settle into residence at the nursing school at least a few weeks before the start of the semester."

"I thought I would still live here."

"Oh no, my dear, being in residence is very much a part of the experience. Besides, it's not as if you're going to be attending nursing school here in Kingston."

"I'm not?"

"Unfortunately, I couldn't arrange that. All their spaces were taken. Instead, I've arranged for you to be in attendance at the Toronto General Hospital. You'll be moving to Toronto."

"But—but..."

"The room off the kitchen will remain your room. We'll expect you back for holidays and during the summer, and perhaps we can even arrange for some of your practical nursing studies to take place at Kingston General."

"I don't know what to say."

"I know, you're hesitant about leaving your young man behind, but Kingston and Toronto are only a train ride apart," she said. "As they say, absence makes the heart grow fonder."

I *was* thinking about David—and my father. One could come and visit me. The other couldn't. But why should I care? He was a drowning man. Besides, he was the one who'd said the most important thing was for me to get away from here. If that was true, he should be happy for me. Besides, Toni was in Toronto, and so was Joe—somewhere. This was going to be like moving *to* family, not *away* from them.

"Is there something more we should talk about?" Mrs. Remington said.

"No, ma'am."

"Is there anything else you want to say?" she asked.

"Just thank you. What you're doing will change my life."

A funny expression came over her face, as if she wanted to say something, something serious. Instead, she just nodded, gave my hands a squeeze and then released them.

Twenty-Eight

I CHEWED ON the end of the pen. That was almost the only action it had seen. I'd scribbled down a few words and the only thing that had accumulated was a bunch of crumpled papers in the waste basket. I heard the door creak and thought it was Mrs. Meyers. I turned around. It was Edward.

"Still up, I see," he said.

I pulled my robe a little tighter. "I was just about to turn out the light and go to sleep."

"Well, don't do that until I leave," he joked.

He came toward me. There was something about the way he was moving, as if he was unsteady on his feet. He came close, too close, brushing against me as he sat on the edge of the desk, and I knew why he was unsteady—I could smell it on his breath. He'd been drinking, and I suddenly felt anxious. I tried to edge away but couldn't move.

"I heard you were at the jail today, visiting that…that *man*."

I nodded my head ever so slightly.

"You shouldn't go. It's wrong. It dishonors your mother's memory. He's a bad man, an *evil* man."

"He told me he's innocent."

He laughed. It was a hard, loud laugh that frightened me. "Even if he was innocent of the murder—which he isn't—he's guilty of something just as bad. That man forced himself upon your mother."

"She told you that?"

"She didn't have to. There is no way, ever, that she would have been with somebody like him of her own free will. Your mother was so innocent, so pure, so good, and he just…"

He suddenly reached out and grabbed both of my wrists with his hands. There was a strange look in his eyes, as if he wasn't even there.

"What are you doing?" I said, now afraid.

"It would have been easy for him to grab her the way I'm grabbing you. She would have been powerless to fight him off, the same way you are powerless to fight me off. What chance did she have?"

"You're hurting me," I said.

"Jail isn't punishment enough for him…to have despoiled someone as special, as innocent, as your mother. I should have just killed him when I had the chance. If I'd done that, she would have lived."

"Please…please, let me go," I whimpered.

He looked at me then, and his expression changed, as if he was seeing me for the first time. He released my wrists and got up from the desk. He started coughing—no, he wasn't coughing, he was crying. Deep sobs from the depth of his chest.

"It's all my fault," he said. "If only I could have stopped it...if only I could have convinced her...if only..."

"You did the best you could," I said. "I know you did the best you could."

"I loved your mother. We *all* loved your mother." He tried to sniff back the tears. "I'm so sorry. I don't know what came over me...so upset...the grief. I'm deeply embarrassed. It was wrong of me to do that. I suppose I wanted you to feel the fear that your mother must have felt. Please don't tell anybody what happened, I beg of you."

"I won't." I wouldn't even know what to say.

"You have to stay away from him," Edward said. "Promise me you'll never go there again."

I thought about saying yes, but I couldn't. "He's my father."

"He's a bad man. Your mother is dead because of him."

"He said he didn't do it, that he was framed."

"Framed?" He paused. "And does he have an idea of who framed him?"

I shook my head.

"But still, you believe him, don't you?"

"I don't know. I just don't know."

"Maybe he thinks I'm responsible," Edward said.

"Why would he think that?"

"Maybe because that's how I feel. If only I could have convinced her to stay here, to stay away from him, to allow me to protect her. I am guilty of not doing enough, not doing what was needed. I hope *you* understand."

"I guess I do. Thank you for trying to help my mother. I know you're just trying to help me too." I paused. "But I can't walk away. Would my mother have walked away?"

"If she had, she would have lived," Edward said. "I have to go. Again, I'm so sorry. Good night."

He left abruptly, leaving me alone except for the extra thoughts crowding my already overworked head. Sleep was not going to happen. Not now and maybe not for the whole night. I had to think, and the best way to do that was to go for a walk.

⟳

As quiet as a church mouse, I tiptoed across the kitchen to the door. Everybody else was long ago asleep, and I didn't want to wake them. I didn't want to talk to anybody. I opened and then closed the door quietly, allowing it to kiss the frame. The air was cool, and I took a deep breath. I could feel it going down into my lungs, filling them up. It felt fresh, new, different than the air inside the house.

I took a few steps along the pathway, and my footfalls echoed off the building. I stepped off the path and onto the grass. I was able to move silently, but the thick dew quickly soaked through my shoes. Fog swirled all around me, and I welcomed it. It gave me a place to hide.

As I opened the back gate, it creaked loudly. I looked around, wondering if anybody had heard. There was nobody around to hear. The world was asleep. It was just me and the night and the fog. Overhead, most of the stars were blurry. The moon was big and full, bright enough to help me find my way along the street. If only life was that simple. If only there was something to help me find my way through the decisions I had to make.

The houses that I could see—set back from the street and often at least partially blocked by hedges and walls— were all dark. Everybody was inside and asleep. I didn't have a destination, but as I walked, I realized I was going in a particular direction, being drawn like a magnet toward the house where it had happened. This was madness. Why would I want to go back there, especially at night and by myself? It made no sense, but still I made the turns to take me in that direction, almost as if my body was moving me there against my will.

I thought back to all the times at the orphanage when I couldn't sleep and I'd go out at night and walk the lanes and country roads and fields. I was so familiar with the paths that I could have found my way with my eyes closed. In the middle of the night it was always calm. I was always calm.

I saw the haze of headlights coming toward me through the fog, which seemed to be getting thicker as I got closer to the lake. The rumble of the engine preceded the arrival of the car. I edged slightly over to the side as it got closer and then zoomed by me, the breeze blowing away the mist that swirled and swallowed up the car. Bright white head-lights were replaced by the dull red glow of taillights, which quickly faded and disappeared. It left me in a darkness that seemed even deeper than before.

I kept moving, gaining speed until I wasn't walking anymore but almost running. I just wanted to get there, my body fighting to maintain the forward momentum, trying to arrive before my head had the strength to turn me around. I came to another intersection, started across and then stopped in the middle of the road. I wasn't sure where I was. I looked around. I couldn't see very far, but I could make out the street signs—Charles and Montreal. I'd arrived. I had been so lost in my thoughts that I'd almost walked right by it.

I stared at the little house. That was where we'd last been together, my mother and I. That was the place my mother had chosen as a refuge, a place to be safe. Safe hadn't happened. A shudder went through my body that had nothing to do with the damp, cool night air. I looked at the house, hoping somehow it could tell me what happened. I wanted to travel back in time to that night to save her—or at least to find out what had really happened. The house remained silent and dark.

Now what would I do? The truth wasn't going to be revealed by my remaining. I needed to leave. To just turn around, retrace my route and get home.

I heard a car engine, but I couldn't see headlights coming from any direction—and then I heard the squeal of tires and caught a blur of movement off to my left as a car moved away from the curb. The dark shadow of a car shot through the fog, pushing it aside and heading toward me. I stepped backward out of its way, but it swerved toward me, and I jumped back again as the car raced by, brushing against the side of my leg.

Suddenly I was in the air, spinning, and it was like everything was moving in slow motion in the dark and the fog. Dreamlike I flew through the air, and then the dream was replaced by the thud of my body against the pavement, pain exploding through my body. I rolled and rolled until I came to a stop.

I lay there, the air knocked out of my lungs, too stunned and shocked to move. My mind spun, trying to make sense of it. A car had come out of nowhere and hit me. Why had I been in the center of the road? I was still on the road. What if another car came by? I forced myself to flip onto my knees and crawl away, bumping up and onto the sidewalk, feeling safe—and then I heard the sound of a car again.

I pushed myself to my feet. There was a low cement wall marking the boundary of the property I was in front of, kitty-corner from my old house. I climbed over the wall and dropped down onto the grass. The wall was now my protection.

Anxiously I scanned the road, looking for the car I could hear. I could see nothing, and then the dark outline of a car with its headlights off became vaguely visible through the fog. It had to be the same car that had brushed against me. Was it coming back because the driver realized how close he'd come to hitting me and wanted to see if I needed assistance...or was it something different? Was he coming back to finish the job he'd started? Why else would he have swerved right into me? Why were the headlights still not on?

I dropped flat to the ground, hidden by the wall. The engine noise got louder as the car came closer, so I didn't dare peek over. I wanted to see the car, try to see the driver, but I couldn't risk it. I pressed myself tight against the wall, lying stretched out, trying to be as still and invisible as possible. The engine noise faded, and then there was nothing. It had gone. I started to get up and then realized there could be another explanation. The car might be pulled over to the side, the engine turned off and the driver sitting there, waiting for me to move, to become visible. What if he had a gun or a knife...or a hammer?

I slumped back down. I wanted to run away, I wanted to scream, but I couldn't. There was only one thing to do. I'd wait it out, even if it meant not moving until morning.

Twenty-Nine

I AWOKE WITH a start, for an instant not knowing where I was, and then it all came back. Anxiously I looked around. I saw nothing except flower beds and the house. My back was still against the wall. I was damp, almost wet, as the dew had settled onto me as I slept. I couldn't believe I'd been able to sleep, but I had—fitfully, fighting against sleep repeatedly until it had finally captured me.

I flexed my arms and drew my legs up, not to fight the chill but to get blood flowing again, so I could move. I had to move. I turned around, pushed myself up slightly and peeked over the top of the wall. It was still dark, but there was a hint of sun to the east. It wasn't morning yet, but it wasn't night anymore either. The sun was getting ready to push above the horizon and announce the day.

The street was deserted. No people and no moving cars, not even any parked at the side of the street. I was alone in the middle of a sleeping city. The darkness was being quickly swallowed up, and I still wanted someplace to hide. Part of me wanted to stay right there, hidden behind the wall forever. That wasn't an option.

Tentatively I got to my feet. My right leg felt sore—the place where the car had brushed against me. If it had been a foot farther over, it wouldn't have been a bruising but a break, maybe worse. What would have happened if I'd still been on that road when he came back, either unconscious or unable to get out of the way?

With each step I felt a little sting go up my leg. I was positive it couldn't be broken, but it wasn't right either. Looking down, I could see where my pants had been torn, and there was a dark stain around the tear—blood. If only David was here with his first-aid kit. Wait. David only lived a few blocks from here. I'd never been to his house, but I knew the block and I could look for his car parked in the drive. That would work. Assuming he was home.

Coming up to the first intersection, I hesitated and looked long and hard in both directions. Nothing. Still, I moved across as quickly as possible, practically dragging my hurt leg behind me as I jumped up onto the sidewalk.

Off to the side, one of the houses had its lights on, a soft glow coming out of the windows. Somebody was up. That made me feel better. I wasn't completely alone. If I had to, I could run to that house, pound on the door, scream for help.

As quickly as I could, I made my way, crossing two more streets before I turned and headed down David's street.

I walked along the first block, checking out cars and drive-
ways, but didn't see anything. Some of the places had a
long lane running down the side, with a garage at the back.
What if his house had a garage and he'd put his car in there
for the night?

I moved into the next block, and up ahead I saw a car
that could be his. It was the same model and about the same
color as David's car, but I couldn't be certain. Should I just
wait to see if he'd come out or risk knocking on the door of
a stranger? I had to chance it. I summoned my strength,
straightened my coat and ran my fingers through my hair to
try to flatten it. How silly, wanting to look my best after all
that I'd gone through!

I reached out to knock and the door popped open.
I jumped backward in shock.

"Lizzy, what are you doing here?" David exclaimed.

I opened my mouth, but no words came out.

"What happened? Are you all right?"

My whole body shuddered and then seemed to shake
the words out. In one long sentence I blurted out the whole
story—from the offer of school to the visit from Edward and
finally to the car almost running me over. The whole thing
sounded so wild and fantastic that I hardly believed what I
was saying. If he hadn't thought I was crackers before, what
would he think now?

He slipped an arm around my waist and ushered me
into the house, practically placing me onto a chair.

"I can see your leg is cut—again—but I want to make sure nothing else more serious is wrong," David said. "Being hit by a car is a serious thing."

He took my left arm and ran his hands up and down, touching, poking, moving my arm in and out and twisting it slightly. "Does any of this hurt?"

"Nothing. No."

"Part of being a cop is you get a little first-aid training," he said.

He did the same with my right arm, and again it all seemed fine except for a little tenderness at the elbow. Next he went to my left leg, starting at the foot and moving up until he was working my knee in and out. I had a little soreness in the knee but only a little. Finally he started to work on the right leg, and I jumped in pain.

"Wait here, and don't move."

He disappeared into what looked like the kitchen. I heard him rummaging around, cutlery clattering loudly. He came back holding a large pair of scissors in his hand.

"What are those for?" I asked.

"I'm going to cut off your pant leg to get a better look at what happened."

"You can't do that—it will ruin them!"

"I'm afraid that ship has already sailed. I don't think you can pull them up far enough for me to see where you're hurt, and I assume you wouldn't want to take them off in front of me, so this is our only option."

"I'll try to pull up my pant leg." Slowly I inched it up, carefully working it over the sore spot until it was revealed.

"That doesn't look so bad," David said. "Basically you just reopened what you'd scraped before. I'll clean it up again and put on some disinfectant. You were lucky you weren't killed."

"Do you think he was trying to do that?"

"It could have just been an accident."

"But you think it could have been more, right?" I asked.

"Have you ever poked a hornet's nest with a stick?"

"Of course not."

"Me neither. At least, not before this. I was called into the station a couple of hours after I dropped you off. I didn't know what it was about, but I found out pretty fast. My sergeant, the chief of detectives and the police chief were all there, waiting for me. They asked me what I thought I was doing, investigating a murder case that had been closed more than a decade ago."

"And what did you tell them?"

"I really didn't have to tell them anything, because they already seemed to know everything. They repeated almost word for word some of the comments made in that visit with your father."

"Mrs. Remington knew all about it too," I said. "She said the guard who was in the room is the son of a family they helped."

"That's not surprising. Everybody knows everybody in this town."

"So do you think Mrs. Remington told them?"

"Or told her son, who told them. I found out that the police chief was appointed directly by the mayor, despite the fact that he wasn't the most senior or experienced person available. People say he *owes* the mayor."

That was one more example of the power of the Remington family.

"The chief told me that my actions made it look like I doubted and questioned the integrity of the officers who did the investigation and put the whole department in a negative light," David said.

"So that's the end of it," I said.

"I thought maybe it would be, but that was before somebody tried to run down my girlfriend. What I didn't tell them, what you don't even know yet, is that I've been investigating. I found two of the three witnesses who testified at the trial."

"How did you find them so quickly?"

"It wasn't hard. One was still living at the same address, with his parents, and the other was actually sitting in the same bar as on the night of the murder."

"And what did they say? What did they tell you?"

"The one from the bar probably hasn't stopped drinking since then. What he had to say was mostly the ranting of a drunk. I wouldn't trust him to remember last night accurately, let alone a dozen years ago."

"And the other?"

"He's a horse of a different color. About a decade ago he found both God and sobriety, and he's willing to swear on a stack of Bibles that your father was with him that entire time."

"And do you believe him?"

"Just because he's sober now doesn't mean he wasn't drunk then, but still…"

"But if he is telling the truth, if he does remember right, then my father didn't do it, and somebody else did, like the man driving that car or the man who called in to tell the police where to find the hammer."

"You could be right," David said. "There's one other thing that I read in the file. The anonymous phone call was from a woman."

I was stunned. I had assumed it was a man, just as I had assumed it was a man driving the car that hit me. Could it have been a woman who killed my mother and who tried to kill me last night?

"In some ways that makes more sense," David said. "A weapon would more likely be used by a woman."

"But—but—why would a woman do that to my mother?"

"The most likely motive is some sort of love triangle. I asked the witness about other women in your father's life, and apparently he wasn't the most solitary figure."

"What does that mean?"

"There were other women in his life before he met your mother. He gave me a couple of names, and I'm going to try to track them down. It gets a little more complicated when women get married and change their names, but I'll dig into it."

"And after that?"

"Either I find them or I don't. Either way I think it might be time to talk to a lawyer about what could come next."

"What would a lawyer do?" I asked.

"He might be able to put an application before the courts to show why a hearing should be held to present new evidence," David explained.

"That could happen?"

"Anything can happen if you have the funds. We're going to need a good lawyer, and the good ones don't come cheap."

"I have over three hundred dollars in my savings account."

"That's a good start. I can add another two hundred."

"I can't take your money," I said.

"If I really needed money, would you give it to me?"

"Of course."

"Then let me do this. I've got the name of a lawyer in town; he's known as a bit of a maverick. He doesn't like the chief of police and has a reputation for fighting for causes he believes in. I think we can get him to believe in this one. We'll go and talk to him."

"Maybe I should go alone. What would happen if the chief found out you were behind this?"

"I don't think it's a question of *if*, but *when*. No secrets in this town."

"So what will happen?"

"They didn't exactly order me not to investigate, so probably they'll just rip a bigger strip off my back, give me punishment duty, or, if worse comes to worst, they might fire me."

"Fire you! I can't let you risk that. You love your job!"

"I do love my job, but not as much as I care for you," he said.

I felt a surge of electricity flow through my entire body. He took my hands in his.

"I'm going to keep that promise I made to your father. I'm going to take care of you. I'm not going to let anybody harm you, not ever."

I searched my mind for a reply, but none came. I threw my arms around him and squeezed him as hard as I could.

Thirty

DAVID STOPPED THE car near the back gate to the estate. It was still early, and I hoped I could sneak in the back door without anybody noticing.

"You need to be safe," David said. "I don't want you to go anywhere. Stay on the grounds of the estate until I've sorted more of this out."

I nodded in agreement. We'd also agreed I wouldn't tell anybody about the car. We had information that only three people knew: him, me and the driver of the car that hit me.

David turned off the engine. "I'm going to walk you to the gate and watch you get into the house."

"That's not necessary. I'll be all right from here."

"I'm not doing it for you, I'm doing it for me. I have to know that you're safe."

We both climbed out. He circled around and took my hand as we walked.

"You know, it might be better if you leave for Toronto sooner rather than later," he said.

On the ride back, I'd told him all about Mrs. Remington's offer, and he was happy for me, even if it meant I had to leave Kingston.

"I'm not even completely sure I should go."

"You're going to go. It's not that far. I can drive down every week to see you."

We stopped at the gate, embraced and kissed. I wanted that moment to go on forever.

"Be safe," he said as he released me. "I'll be back later tonight, hopefully with some news."

He opened the gate for me, and I started toward the mansion. He remained where he was, watching. Maybe it wasn't necessary, but it certainly felt good.

I looked up at the house. The windows were dark, the curtains drawn. There was no question that Mrs. Remington was still asleep, and the whole household generally didn't start work until just before she rose.

I hesitated at the back door, turned, waved to David, and he waved back. Opening the door, I stepped into the kitchen. All was quiet and the lights were still off. I'd go to my room, get freshened up and change, and nobody would know that I hadn't been here last night.

I caught a glimpse of movement and turned. There was a figure in the darkness in the corner. He stepped forward. Edward!

"Edward, what are—"

He put a finger to his lips to silence me as he walked toward me. "We need to talk," he whispered. "About last night."

"It's all right, I understand—"

"Not here. Come."

He started to walk away. I hesitated. I didn't want to go with him. I didn't want to talk to him about what he had done last night. It wasn't important. I had far bigger concerns. He turned around, looking concerned that I wasn't right behind him, and gestured for me to follow. I had no choice now.

He opened the doorway that led to the servants' stairs. That surprised me. I'd never seen any of the Remingtons on those stairs. I followed him up a flight and then we continued on up to the next floor. Rather than going out into the hall, he reached for a panel that opened to reveal another set of stairs.

"You probably didn't know about this set, did you?" he asked.

"No, I didn't."

"My brother and I explored all the secret passages as children. This house is full of surprises."

I felt surprised and, more than that, concerned. Where was he leading me?

We continued up; it looked as if the stairs dead-ended at the top. Then there was a sound as a panel slid open to reveal a set of curtains. He pushed them aside, and we entered a room where I'd never been.

Everything was still and dark. Little bits of light were starting to force their way in through the drawn shades. The furnishings were covered with sheets, and there was a thick, stale feel to the air. I could almost taste the dust.

"Thanks for coming up here to talk," Edward said. He gave me a big smile that made me feel a bit more comfortable. "I wanted to talk without waking anybody else up. I felt it was necessary for us to have a private conversation."

He gestured for me to sit down. I took a seat on a couch covered by a sheet, and he pulled up a chair and sat down right in front of me. I was sure I knew what he wanted to talk about. I wanted to get the conversation started so I could get it over with.

"I'm not going to talk to anybody about what happened," I said. "You don't need to apologize to me again."

"Me apologize to you?" he questioned. "I think you owe me an apology."

"Me? Why?"

"For keeping me waiting all night. Is it your habit to be out all night?"

"No, of course not!"

"Were you with him?" he asked.

"Him...my father?"

"Of course not!" he snapped. "That *man* you're seeing."

"David drove me home this morning."

"Did he take advantage of you?" he demanded.

"No, of course not!"

"You look disheveled—your clothing, your hair."

"Something happened," I explained.

"I'm sure *many* things happened, but that's not why I need to talk to you. I need you to be honest with me. Can you be honest?"

I nodded.

"Honesty is important. Your father—do you, in your heart, believe that he is innocent?"

I didn't answer.

"Well? Do you or don't you?"

"I don't know."

"Do you think my brother did it?" he demanded.

"No, I don't."

"Good, because I *know* he didn't do it. But still you think somebody else murdered your mother, and that your father is innocent. Why would you believe that?" he asked.

"There were witnesses who said he wasn't there."

"Discredited witnesses who lied for him!"

"David doesn't think they lied."

"And do you believe that?" he asked.

"I'm not sure, and I need to be sure. We need to find out."

"Do you have a plan?" Edward asked.

"We're thinking that maybe we should get a lawyer for him."

"To bring it back before the courts? To appeal the conviction?"

I nodded.

He got to his feet and walked over to the window, parting the curtains slightly, allowing more light to stream in. He turned back around.

"In this light I could almost believe your mother is sitting there instead of you. She often came up here with me. You wouldn't know that, of course. *Nobody* knew that. You and your mother are so similar in so many ways, right down to your poor judgment when it comes to men."

"What do you mean?"

He let out a big sigh. "I loved your mother."

"Everybody did."

"Not that way," he snapped. "I loved her. I genuinely loved her. If only she'd listened, none of this would have happened. I was willing to be with her, support her, raise you as my own daughter. Possibly even someday take her as my wife."

I gasped.

He shook his head. "It all would have been so different. You would have been raised as the stepdaughter of Edward Remington. Your mother would have been cared for, her every need provided for, your every need provided for."

My mind raced, thinking about all that could have been, and all that was instead.

"But she wouldn't listen. It is so sad that it all has come down to this."

What did he mean?

He pulled a pistol out of his coat.

"What are you doing?"

"You couldn't leave well enough alone, could you?" he asked. "You had to stir up trouble. Get up!" he yelled.

Before I could answer, he had grabbed my arm and yanked me to my feet.

"Now I'm going to have to take care of you," he hissed. "The way I took care of your mother."

"You're the one who...?"

He nodded his head. "Really, she did it to herself. If she'd listened to me, it all could have been different."

"But why? Why did you do it?"

"She rejected me, told me to leave...and then..." He shook his head. "It was all a blur, so fast, as if it wasn't happening, and she started to scream. I had to stop her. I had the hammer with me, just in case *he* was there."

"You won't get away with this," I stammered.

"I have once and I will again. It would have been so much better if you'd left the whole thing alone, so much easier if you hadn't jumped out of the way last night."

"That was you in the car?"

"Of course! And now I have to finish off what I started."

"If you fire the gun, everybody will hear," I said.

"Do you think I need a gun to kill you?" he questioned. "I could do it with—"

The door to the room opened, and Mrs. Remington peeked inside.

"Mrs. Remington!" I yelled. "Help me, help me!"

"Keep her quiet!" Mrs. Remington ordered.

What did she say?

"Somebody will hear," she said as she stepped into the room and closed the door behind her. "Keep the girl quiet!"

Suddenly Edward put a hand around my throat, squeezing tightly. He pulled me so close I could feel his breath against me. "If you yell again, I will kill you here and now. Do you understand?"

I nodded, and he released his grip. I practically fell over, barely managing not to tumble backward as I gulped in a breath of air.

"You know, Mother, none of this would have been necessary if you hadn't arranged to bring her back here," he said.

"She was coming to Kingston anyway. I simply wanted to be able to have more control, and, as always, it's a good thing I did. I'm here to help clean up your mess once again."

Then it dawned on me. "You were the one who made the phone call about where to find the hammer."

"Arranged all the details and then made the phone call," she said. "I told you, dear, a mother will do whatever is necessary to protect her children. Edward, do you have a plan?"

"Yes. I know it's not enough to dispose of her without disposing of her boyfriend."

"David? What are you talking about?" I demanded.

"You're right," Mrs. Remington said. "He asks too many questions. But how you will get him out of the picture?"

"It's simple. Instead of him asking questions, I plan to make him the answer. It will be such a sad story: our dear Lizzy was killed by her boyfriend, and then he was so distraught that he took his own life."

"That's impossible. He would never harm me...never take his own life."

"Of course he wouldn't," Mrs. Remington said. "Which is why we'll arrange it. It shouldn't happen here at the house."

"It won't," Edward said. "I was thinking east of town, by the lake. I'll call and arrange a meeting, tell him that Lizzy needs his help."

"I'll make the call. He'll believe me and, perhaps more important, he is afraid of me," Mrs. Remington said. "He won't suspect a thing. Now, first things first. We need to get her out of the house. I'll go down to the kitchen and summon all the staff for a meeting, although they'll want to know where Lizzy is."

"Have somebody check her room, and they'll see she isn't there," Edward said. "It will only help to have them know she's missing."

"Wait here. I'll be back," Mrs. Remington said. "And keep her quiet!"

She made her way to the door, felt around for the handle and opened it. Richie was standing there.

"What are you doing?" Richie asked.

"Nothing, nothing," she stammered. "You have to go downstairs."

He looked past his mother, first at Edward and then at me. "Lizzy, would you like to come out to see my pigeons?"

"She can't come. She and Edward are talking," Mrs. Remington said. She was composed again, hardly missing a beat.

"Edward can come too."

"I haven't got time for this!" Edward snapped.

"Come on, Richie," Mrs. Remington said. "It's time for us to—" Richie stepped into the room, brushing by his mother and almost knocking her down as he passed. He was, as always, holding his shovel.

"Get him out of here!" Edward yelled.

Richie stepped between Edward and me, stopping with his face just inches away from mine. He looked confused, almost pained, as he stared directly into my eyes. His mother yelled and his brother grabbed him by the shoulder, trying to move him, but Richie shrugged him off, standing immobile.

"Are you scared?" he asked me.

I nodded my head.

"Did my brother hurt you?" he asked.

Before I could answer he spun around until he was facing Edward. "Did you make Lizzy cry? Did you hurt her?"

"Get away, you big oaf!" Edward yelled. He went to raise his pistol, and Richie swung his shovel. There was a dull, sickening thud as it smashed into Edward's head. Edward flew backward, and then his body crumpled to the floor.

"What happened?" Mrs. Remington screamed. "What is happening?" She fumbled forward, unable to see clearly what had transpired. "Edward, Edward, where are you?"

She bumped into Richie and then practically tripped over Edward, lying at her feet in a ball. Realizing it was her son, she dropped to her knees and felt around until she found his head, which was bleeding badly. His eyes opened, and he started to groan. He was conscious and alive. I had to get away before he could get up. I had to get away.

Then I saw it. Right over by Mrs. Remington's side was the pistol, lying on the floor. I could run, but how far could I get? I jumped forward, grabbed the gun and raced to the door. I held the gun out in front of me, trying to pretend I knew what I was doing.

"I have the gun. It's over. I'm going to call the police," I said, trying to sound as calm as possible.

"Call the police," Mrs. Remington said. "The sooner they get here, the sooner you'll be arrested."

"Arrested?"

"For attempted murder. You tried to kill my son! You hit him—you did this!"

"I didn't do anything. I'll tell them the truth."

"The truth is whatever I tell them it is," she said. "Who do you think they're going to believe—me and my son, or you? Do you think our dear friend the chief of police is going to do what *I* ask or what *you* want?"

I was shocked. Too shocked to even know what to say in response, but I knew she was probably right. Somehow, this was all going to be my fault; nobody would believe me.

"It wasn't Lizzy, it was me," Richie said.

"They're not going to get a chance to hear what he has to say," Mrs. Remington said. "I'll make sure of that."

"They will believe me." Mrs. Meyers pushed through the curtains. I couldn't have been more shocked if a ghost had appeared.

"You don't understand what happened," Mrs. Remington said. "This girl assaulted my son, she pulled that weapon on us and—"

"I heard everything. I heard the *truth*," Mrs. Meyers said. "I know exactly what happened, and there's no need to call the police because they've already been called. I sent Nigel to do that."

In the background I thought I heard something—a siren. Then it got louder, joined by a second and possibly a third. The police *were* coming.

Mrs. Meyers turned to look right at me. "I'm not going to let anybody hurt *our* Lizzy ever again."

Thirty-One

"DO YOU THINK it's going to be much longer?" I asked.

"I'm not sure," David said. "Just be patient. It's only a few minutes past one."

He was sitting on the fender of his car and motioned for me to join him, which I did.

"Enjoy the sun and savor the moment," he said. "Just close your eyes and drink in the sun."

"I'm afraid to close my eyes in case when I open them this will all have been nothing more than a dream."

"It's real," he said. "*I'm* real, and I'm not going anywhere. Ever."

He took my hand in his, intertwining my fingers with his. This was both the most real and the most unreal part of everything that had happened. In the short space of three weeks, there had been a rush of events, starting with the arrival of the police and followed by the arrest of both Mrs. Remington and Edward, the forced resignation of the chief of police and an investigation of all their crimes. I had left the estate and found a new place to live, and then there was the appeal of my father's case in court. Being here, waiting, was the final scene.

"There's one thing I still don't understand," I said. "Why did you do all of this?"

"That's a silly question. I did it for you."

"But you hardly knew me," I said.

"That's where you're wrong. I haven't known you for long, but that doesn't mean I don't know you well." He paused. "Lizzy, I know you, and that 'not knowing you for long' business, well, time will take care of that. I'm planning on fixing that one day at a time for a long, long time."

He always seemed to not only know the right thing to say, but actually said it—and more important—he meant it.

"I don't know how I ever got so lucky," I said.

"First off, I'm the lucky one, and second, I think it was only a matter of time until your luck evened out. You went through so much, and you didn't just survive, but you grew and flourished and kept moving forward. You became somebody special, somebody I'm not planning to let go."

I tightened my grip on his hand. I wasn't letting him go either.

"I have to admit, there were times when I thought this whole thing with your father was going nowhere. And then there was a moment when I thought it would have been wise to just let it go, forget about it, do what the chief was telling me to do, but I couldn't." He paused. "I had to try to be as brave and strong as you."

"Me?"

"You're one of the strongest, bravest people I've ever met."

"You have no idea just how scared I was sometimes." And I meant for many years, long before all of this started.

"It isn't about not being scared. Everybody gets scared. It's about still doing what needs to be done in spite of being afraid. That's what makes you so brave."

"I don't know about that."

"I do. I do, and...look, I think it's time. It's happening."

The big black metal gate of the prison swung open. Two men, one in uniform and the other in a suit, emerged. The one in the suit was my father. The two shook hands, and then my father took a few steps, stopped and looked around. He saw us parked across the street from the prison, and he waved.

I jumped off the fender and took a step, then stopped. David was still sitting on the car.

"Aren't you coming?" I asked.

He shook his head. "Just you."

I understood why, but I still felt scared—and brave enough to go.

"Go on," David said. "Go to your father."

I took a step and then another and then I found myself running, tears flowing, and I met him in the middle of the street, and he hugged me and I hugged him.

"Thank you, thank you so much...for everything, for being here," he said.

I tried to speak, but I couldn't get any words to come out.

"You *are* my little angel," my father said.

ERIC WALTERS began writing in 1993 as a way to entice his fifth-grade students into becoming more interested in reading and writing. Since then he has published ninety novels and picture books. He has won more than a hundred awards, and his bestselling novels have been translated into more than a dozen languages.

Eric writes in a variety of genres, and his stories often reflect his background in education and social work and his commitment to humanitarian and social-justice issues. Over the past few years he has been the driving force behind the Creation of Hope (www.creationofhope.com), an organization that serves orphans and needy children in Kenya, and in 2014 he was named a Member of the Order of Canada "for his contribution as an author of literature for children and young adults whose stories help young readers grapple with complex social issues."

Eric lives in Mississauga with his wife, Anita, and they have three grown children. When not writing, or playing or watching sports, he enjoys listening to jazz and eating in fine restaurants featuring drive-through service. For more information, visit www.ericwalters.net.

**Uncover more Secrets—
starting with this excerpt from:**

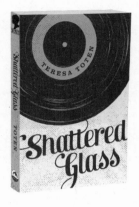

I WAS PERSPIRING so much that my bare feet left footprints on the floor. I was also pacing, which didn't help the sweating thing. Betty had written me weeks ago. It had been forwarded from Loretta's Diner, which had been set up as our postal drop. Joe had let them know my address as soon as he got my first note. I'd torn up five previous attempts. But this time I was going to do it. I was going to write her back. Hence the pacing.

I sat down and devoted the first page to apologizing and asking for forgiveness for A) sneaking away without saying goodbye and B) not writing back sooner. Then I paced some more.

Now my hands were wet.

Things are so unbelievable here in Toronto that I don't know where to begin! It's all good, mainly. Well, actually, it's a bit of a roller coaster, and I'm still having the nightmares.

But still good, you know? All in all, I'm pretty proud of myself. Like, there's a billion people in this city and I even know some of them! I have this amazing huge room, but I'm the only one in it, which is good except when I'm lonely and when I have the dreams.

Anyway, when the dreams are bad (you know, me screaming my head off), a very nice man who is a professor of literature at the University of Toronto comes down and knocks on my door until I wake up and answer it. Isn't that sweet? I live in sort of a rooming house, but it's just me and the professor who board here. Mrs. Grady Vespucci owns 75 Hazelton and she is the most beautiful woman you could possibly imagine, except she drinks a bit too much. She calls them "refreshments" but they're spirits, Betty, no two ways about it. Grady gives me fashion advice and life advice and I tell her most everything when she hasn't over-refreshed.

I wrote her about Big Bob, Mr. Kenyatta, Crying Rachel and even Ethan, but I felt myself heating up even more, so only a word.

Ethan is the son of Mr. Brooks Goldman, who is this amazing musician whose band, the Ramblers, plays at the Purple Onion all the time and who, embarrassingly, I thought was my father for a minute. I also thought that Ian Tyson was my father (same amount of time). Don't ask—it was HUMILIATING! I know, I know...I'm the one that teased you all for your stupid orphan fantasies, but get me out of the orphanage and I become a champion fantasizer! Maybe it's the alone thing. So in the end, unlike you, I haven't made much progress in finding out who my real father is or was, and I haven't tried real hard on the mother front. Actually, I am trying to track a lady down who was her best friend, but it's complicated—she's in a ladies' prison!

I am so glad to hear that you are well settled with people who care about you. I am even gladder to hear that you have a young man! David sounds wonderful and the FIRST KISS sounds spectacular (I'm so, so jealous)!!! I have a young man, too, except he's older, maybe quite a bit older! Cassidy (it has just hit me that I don't know what his last name is!) is a businessman, and he might be almost thirty! I know, I know...But he is SUCH a gentleman, and everybody looks when I'm with him because he is so handsome, and I'm not exaggerating for once. He is going to take me to a very posh party one day, and I'm already fretting about what to wear. He hasn't kissed me yet—as I say, he is a true gentleman. He is very, very interested in my story about being an orphan. He really cares. I believe he will try to help me.

I had to get up and walk around again. Did I sound all braggy about Cassidy? The truth was that he was thrilling and exciting and...he scared me a little. But I liked that too. I hadn't talked about him to Grady, which felt kind of like a lie. Mrs. Hazelton always said that a lie of omission was just as bad as a flat-out whopper. I'd been "omissioning" a lot, and while it didn't used to bother me much with Mrs. Hazelton, I felt guilty about it with Grady.

Anyway, anyway, I miss you to pieces and more. Actually, I miss all of us as an "us" more than I ever thought possible. I dreamed of being away and on my own, of having my own room, for such a long time and now that I finally have it…well, it's just not like I thought it would be is all. Tell your fella I said hi and to treat you like a queen. Good luck at your end with everything, and write me soon if not sooner.

Love you lots,

Toni

xoxox

Okay, so see? This was why I didn't want to write. It all sounded stupid on paper. If only I could see her, talk to her. Here it was, almost August, and I was no closer to finding out anything about who I was or where I came from. All this time I'd thought that I didn't want to know anything about my father or about her. Now, writing about my lack of progress, I truly realized that I did.

I mean, who was I?

Why was I?

A girl's got to know these things.

I folded the letter and shoved it into an envelope and addressed it to Betty's new home.

Home. With a family, a *real* family, to belong to.

I showered and got myself done up in my second new scoop-neck T-shirt, the royal-blue one. Grady approved of it the most. I slunk out of 75 Hazelton. I could hear the professor and Grady speaking softly. They were busy. They didn't need me always barging in on them.

Come to think of it, no one needed me.

Snap out of it! I hated it when people got all droopy drawers, but I especially hated it when I did. So I gave my head a shake, plastered on a big smile and marched to work. Still smiling, I combed the place for Ethan. Even when he was mad at me, Ethan made me feel "real." Besides, I felt awful for taking off on him. As usual, he was fiddling with equipment onstage.

"Hey!"

Nothing.

"Hey, I looked all over for you last night, but I couldn't find you. Look, I'm sorry about..."

Ethan stood up. He was holding a couple of screw-drivers. "Who's the old guy?"

"The old...oh, that's Cassidy. He's a friend."

Ethan nodded. He didn't get all snotty and holier than thou. He looked right at me for a bit and then shook his head. "Okay." He nodded. "I got it." And he walked away.

Wait. What?

"What? Ethan, wait!" But he kept on walking.

The place was filling up fast. I had to start on my tables. "Ethan!" But he did not turn around. And I couldn't figure out why it mattered so much. But it did.

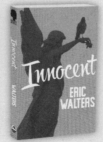